The More Things Change

A Novel

By Elle Nora

Printed in the United States of America

ISBN: 978-0-9910011-6-3

Gratitude

As always, I'm grateful to God for all that He created me to be and to my circle of family and friends for continuing to be the wind beneath my wings.
- Elle Nora

<u>Other Books by Elle Nora</u>

Better Choices

If you would like to join my mailing list, or order my
other books, please visit my website:
www.readellenora.com
or e-mail me: elle@readellenora.com

Chapter 1

Joya's heart raced, and she couldn't breathe. "What is on my chest?" she wondered, feeling a heaviness that she could not identify. She felt a strong wave of nausea and fought with all of her strength not to let it all go. In the darkness, she continued to beg for breath, but it wouldn't come.

She was hot and drenched in her own sweat. "This is not good. Am I dying?" Joya prayed to God for relief. Whatever that was. It could be being able to breathe or actually taking her last breath. Either way, she could not continue to struggle.

She felt peace and relaxed into it. She exhaled. Then inhaled. "Thank you, God." She could breathe again.

She opened her eyes. "How did I get here?" She was in the Georgian Country Club. It was decorated in white and gold. A familiar feeling came over Joya, knowing that she had been there before. She focused her vision on Minister Srene. "Oh. If Srene is here, then everything is ok," she thought.

She looked to her right and saw Troy. The sense of dread that she had just felt caught her again in her chest. Troy looked directly at her and delivered his signature smile. Joya looked into his eyes.

She screamed.

Troy's eyes and his smile had paralyzed her. She couldn't move. Her chest hurt and all she could do was scream while Troy laughed at her.

"Please STOP!" Joya begged. *Troy continued to laugh. He didn't say a word to Joya, but he laughed and kept his eyes on her, never blinking.*

Joya screamed, "TROY!!! STOP IT!!!! NOOOOOOO!!!!"

Someone is calling my name. Who is it? Where are they? Please save me! Get me away from him!

"Joya...Joya! Wake up!" Mona was gently shaking Joya. She heard her sister screaming when she was downstairs preparing breakfast. She had convinced Joya to spend the night at her house. It had been two weeks since Joya's "wedding" and although Joya seemed fine, Mona wanted to spend some time with her.

She'd made up a story to convince Joya to spend the night at her house. She conveniently set up a "surprise" for her long-time partner, William to celebrate a promotion that he had recently received as a one of the top business development executives at his company. He really had received the promotion and Mona was planning a much bigger celebration, but that would come later. She was grateful to William for agreeing to a smaller celebration a little early. He understood Mona's love and protection for her little sister.

Mona asked Joya to come over and help with the 'last-minute' celebration for William and a few of their closest friends. Mona purposely scheduled a late dinner so that she could persuade Joya to spend the night instead of driving home.

Mona and William were very careful not to reveal the biggest part of the promotion and the real reason for the celebration. It was an enjoyable evening with friends and Mona was glad that she decided to do it. Despite the recent events in her life, Joya seemed to have a good time at the dinner party.

Mona continued to gently shake her sister, but she wouldn't wake up. She was soaked in her perspiration and obviously traumatized by whatever had entered her dreams that were now a nightmare. She was trembling, and Mona could hear her rapid heartbeat.

"Get him away from me!" Joya screamed.

"Joya! Wake up!" Mona gently tapped her in a slapping motion on her cheeks. She didn't want to slap her, but she was afraid for her sister. Her thoughts raced back and forth. She was angry with Troy and blamed him for what her sister was going through. But, she didn't want her to have a heart attack right now, so she needed to put her anger on the back burner for now and focus on Joya.

She tapped her cheeks a little harder. Joya opened her eyes. She looked at Mona like she was a stranger at first. Then she recognized the face that she had loved her entire life. It was the face of her big sister that had always been there for her, that she always admired and that had always stepped in for her. She wrapped her arms around Mona's neck, grateful to her, once again, for saving her.

Chapter 2

"Joya. Are you alright? You scared me to death! I was downstairs starting breakfast when I heard you scream." Mona looked at her sister with concern waiting for her answer.

"Yes, I'm fine. Thanks for waking me up from THAT nightmare." Joya realized that her nightshirt was soaking wet. "Ugh! I'm going to jump in the shower and come down to help you with breakfast," Joya said as she jumped from the bed to the floor. She wanted to deflect the conversation away from the nightmare she had just had. She didn't want to give Mona any fuel for her fire against Troy. She had been against the wedding from the beginning.

Mona knew her sister almost as well as she knew herself. She suspected that Joya didn't want to talk about the nightmare that she just had or the real-life nightmare of planning a wedding with someone that she knew she was not going to marry. She would give her time and would be there for Joya when she was ready to talk about it. Hopefully, that time would be today.

"Okay," Mona said. "We'll finish up breakfast when you come downstairs. William left for the gym already. So, it's just us girls!"

"Great," Joya answered, already in the bathroom. She closed the door and started the shower.

Taking off the wet clothes and tossing them aside, she eagerly stepped into the shower, welcoming the warmth of the water. She relaxed into the pulse of the jets, turning around so that the water could massage her neck and back muscles that were still tense from her nightmare. Joya felt like she had been physically beaten in addition to being emotionally exhausted.

She remembered the dream. She closed her eyes and saw Troy piercing her with his eyes and laughing at her. It wasn't far from the truth of what had actually happened. She knew that she had done the right thing. Mona and Sam told her that she had. So did David.

David. What am I going to do about David?

Joya still had to figure out her feelings for David. She appreciated him for what he had done to expose Troy. But, still was not sure how to handle the feelings he had for her. And her feelings for him.

She felt the tears as they soaked her face. She wasn't exactly sure why she was crying, there were so many reasons, but it was a welcomed release. She turned to face the water coming from the showerhead and allowed the water to wash away her tears.

Chapter 3

"That shower felt sooo good," Joya said, trying to sound as normal as possible as she stepped into the kitchen. Mona was starting to prepare omelets in her gourmet kitchen. Joya loved Mona's house. Mona put a lot of time and energy decorating it to perfection. Each room displayed Mona's elegant taste. The kitchen had all upgraded stainless steel appliances, blended with black and silver granite counter tops and coordinated backsplashes.

Joya took her place beside her sister and started chopping the scallions for their omelets. Always emotionally close, the sisters were different sized versions of each other. Mona stood five inches taller over Joya's petite vanilla frame. Joya always envied Mona's beautiful silky black hair and chestnut complexion inherited from their mother, Delia. Joya was almost the exact same size as their mother, but Delia had always told her that she had her father's features. Mona had gotten her height from their father, Louis. Although the sisters had strong characteristics that were obvious from each parent, it was uncanny how much they looked alike.

There was a moment of silence before Mona asked, "Are you really okay? That was some nightmare that you had."

"I'm fine. That was the first time that I dreamed about it. Maybe, because I was sleeping here and not in my own bed."

"Yeah. Right. That's it. Not sleeping in your bed caused you to scream out, and sweat like that. Your heart almost beat out of your chest!"

That's Mona. Always exaggerating, Joya thought. But, she knew that her sister always had her best interest. If she had only listened to her instead of her heart when Troy proposed…

"I know. You are right - as usual." Joya gave her sister a loving nudge. "I guess it was time to dream about that snake. But, I don't have any regrets about how I handled the situation."

Mona finished cooking the omelets and took their plates to the table already set in the morning room. The sun was perfectly shining through the floor to ceiling windows. They took their seats at the white and gray marble top dinette that looked out onto the garden.

Mona cut into her omelet and took a bite. She had to ask, "How did you get through it? Why didn't you tell me what was going on?" Deciding to make light of it, which might prompt Joya to open up, she said, "It would have saved me the embarrassment of fainting at your wedding had I known what you were planning."

They laughed together at the memory of Mona fainting at the Country Club when Joya announced that she was not going to marry Troy.

Joya had to focus on swallowing so that she would not choke on the tea that she had just sipped. "I know, girl. I am so sorry," she laughed. "I knew that you would be dramatic, you get that from Ma, but I was not prepared to see you go down like that!"

Mona chuckled, "It was such a shock, but I quickly recovered. I got THAT from Ma, too." They laughed again, each with loving memories of their sweet Delia running through their minds and hearts.

Joya brought her attention back to the questions that her sister had just posed. It was time to come clean with Mona. About everything.

Chapter 4

Joya told Mona about the fateful and life changing night that she left her phone on her desk and what she had overheard when she returned to retrieve it. Mona gasped and stopped eating when Joya recounted what she had heard Troy say on the telephone. Although she had only heard his side of the conversation, the sisters were in agreement in their assessment of Troy's actions.

"Did Sam know?"

"No," Joya answered honestly. "I was so angry and hurt, but I knew that I had to get into fighting mode. I was NOT about to be played for a fool by the likes of Troy." Her voice caught in her throat, "I just couldn't believe that he could be so cruel and do that to me."

Before Mona could console her, she recovered and continued, "I planned the rest of the wedding with a vengeance. I was so hurt and humiliated, but I had to pull all the strength that I had to keep up the front. Can you imagine what it was like ordering flowers, working with the caterers and all of the STUFF that goes with planning a wedding knowing that it was really not going to happen? The worst part was being in Troy's presence, pretending that everything was fine. I slept next to him at night with one eye open."

Joya continued, "I knew that confronting Troy one-on-one would have no impact, but a public humiliation would. Putting him on blast the way that I did was the only way. He needed to be exposed for what he is. Had I told you or Sam, you would have talked me out of it." She smiled at Mona when she said it, believing it to be true.

Mona digested what her sister had just shared with her. *I wish that she had come to me so that I could have helped her through it. How did she do it?* "You are probably right. I probably would have advised you against going through all of that planning and expense. I had no idea what you were dealing with." Then remembering her statement to Joya when they were shopping for dresses for the wedding, she said, "I did tell you how I felt about your choice of Troy as your husband." She said it without accusation so that her sister would accept it with the loving spirit in which it was being given.

"I know. I just wanted to be in a relationship so badly that I couldn't see beyond Troy's handsomeness, his smile and charm," she said letting out a long breath.

Mona was curious. "What did you whisper in his ear that day? It was right before he gathered his posse and walked away."

Joya laughed and thought for a second whether or not she should share what she had said to Troy with her sister. Mona was such an elegant woman, always careful about what she said and how she said it. *What the hell?* She told Mona exactly what she had whispered to Troy.

Mona screamed, "Oh NO! You did NOT!" But, she had to laugh with her sister. Troy deserved it. He deserved that and more.

"I know that I should not have said it, which is why I whispered it instead of saying to so everyone could hear it. I was so hurt, and I kept hearing him bragging about 'putting it down' with me like he was genuinely concerned about pleasing me. He never even asked me anything about how I felt." Joya went on to tell Mona about a quickie that she and Troy had at her office.

Mona screamed again, "Way too much information! I may NEVER go into your conference room again!" Joya laughed at her elegant sister, glad that she was able to share with her like this. She was feeling better, so she decided to totally open up with Mona.

"Do you remember David from the wedding? He was the guy that was in the dressing room when you and Sam came to check on me after the wedding."

"Yes. I do remember him. I thought it was strange that he was there with you, but Sam told me that he was a friend of yours."

Joya told Mona how she had met David and how he had helped her with her business. "He has been a good friend. He wants to take me on a vacation next week. He says that I need just to go somewhere and decompress."

"Really now? Mona said, interested in this David person. "Where are you two going?"

"I'm not sure. He's planning everything. I just need to 'show up.' That's refreshing after being with a 'scab' like Troy." Mona laughed at her sister's analogy.

Joya continued, "I'm not sure how I feel about vacationing with him after everything that just went down. I'm not depressed. I don't feel anything."

Needing to know more about David, Mona pressed, "So, what type of relationship do you have with this guy and why am I just hearing about him?" Mona was now in accelerated protective mode, sensing there was something about David that Joya was not sharing. Especially, since she had not heard of him before.

"As I said, he has really been there for me. You may not remember, but he came to Mother's funeral. Troy didn't even come. He has a good job, and he cares for me."

Exhaling, Joya decided to be totally honest with her sister. What did she have to lose? "He's married."

Mona inhaled, held her breath and held her stare at Joya. Just then William walked in. William and Mona had been together for over ten years. They didn't live together, but they spent the weekends together and had keys to each other's home. Joya always thought that they should just live together, but Mona was not the 'shacking up' type, not that she judged anyone else that made that decision. It just wasn't for her.

Mona exhaled, turned to William and exchanged a look of silent communication with him. He understood.

"Hey, ladies! Did I miss breakfast?"

"Hey, Sweetie. No, we saved you some. Sit down while I cook your omelet," Mona said getting up from the table. It was her turn to experience tightness in the chest.

I'm going to have to wait until another time to share our big news with Joya. Now is definitely not the time.

Chapter 5

"Hey pretty lady," David said when Joya answered her cell phone.

Glad to hear from him, Joya smiled into the phone, "Hey, handsome!" *He is going to want my answer today.*

"What are you up to today?" he asked. He was in his car, driving to pick up his son from football practice.

"I just left my sister's house; running some errands," Joya answered. She didn't want to see him today. She was still recovering from the emotions of the nightmare.

She anticipated his next question, so she offered, "I thought about what you asked me. I appreciate your offer to take me on vacation."

David held his breath waiting for her to continue. By her tone, he could not determine what her answer would be. He cared so much for Joya, although his situation did not appear ideal for a relationship, he was willing to do whatever it took to make it work with Joya. This trip was the first step to demonstrate that to her. *Please say that you will go with me!*

Joya paused for a moment of deliberate effect. "When do we leave and where are we going?"

"YES!" David screamed into the phone. He pumped the air with his fist. Joya's answer had made him extremely happy. He looked forward to spending time with her to show her the type of man that he is and the type of relationship that they could have together. She deserved a man that was honest, trustworthy and that genuinely cared for her – not that snake, Troy. David despised Troy for the type of person that he was and what he had done to Joya.

Joya smiled at his reaction. It gave her a warm feeling knowing how much David cared for her. *If he just wasn't married. What would Mommy think? Oh my God! And what would Daddy think?* Based on the look Mona had given her earlier this morning, she knew that she was not pleased. Too late, she had already made her decision.

Joya released herself from her thoughts to focus on what David was saying. "It's a surprise where we are going, but we leave in two weeks. I will take care of EVERYTHING. You just be packed and ready. I'll pick you up from your house and drive us to the airport. Don't worry about ANYTHING. Joya, I'm so glad that we will have some private time together. You deserve to be spoiled, and I'm going to do that for you."

"David…"

Anticipating what she was going to say, David interjected, "Joya, I have no expectation, and there is no pressure on you, okay? We will be in a suite with separate bedrooms. You will have your own room. I totally respect you and won't do anything to destroy that."

What a breath of fresh of air. "Thanks, David. I'm glad that you understand. I'm looking forward to it." Wanting to lighten the conversation, Joya asked, "How should I pack? I don't know what type of clothes I'll need since you won't disclose our destination," she said jokingly.

David laughed. "Bring lots of bikinis!"

"Just kidding!" He quickly said so that Joya would not change her mind. "Pack for tropical weather, which will include swimwear of your choice. And don't worry. If you need something after we arrive, we'll buy it!" David liked to shop almost as much as Joya did.

Appreciating the humor and looking forward to the trip, Joya told David that she would be prepared accordingly to his suggestions. They both had a full Saturday ahead of them, so they agreed to talk after the weekend. After they hung up, David continued to drive with a huge smile on his face, thinking of Joya and his plans for their trip together. It had been a long time since he had been this happy. If ever.

I love her so much.

Chapter 6

Sunday Brunch with Sam was always a treat for Joya. They decided to meet at one of their favorite restaurants, Potomac View. Joya had not been there since that fateful day of running into Troy, but she was ready to suck it up and move on. Going to Potomac View would be cathartic. Being there with her best friend, Sam would make it worth the effort.

True to Joya's expectation, Sam entered the restaurant like she always does: like a whirlwind. Always capturing attention with her full-figured brown frame, beautiful face and haute couture, she walked through the main dining room of the restaurant and joined Joya on the outside deck.

Joya had made reservations for them to be seated outside and had prayed for good weather. She and Sam loved dining alfresco and especially enjoyed Potomac View where they could see the air traffic in and out of Washington National Airport.

Joya stood to hug her friend when she saw her approach the table. "Hey, girl! Look at you in all of your 'diva-ness!' I am absolutely loving that color on you!"

Sam was styling her latest designer two-piece pants outfit in rich coral with gold accents. Sam always dressed to capture attention and she did not fail this time, as many ladies on the deck had focused their attention to admire her.

Although not trying to compete, Joya had her share of the attention in her fitted silver dress that perfectly flattered her petite, shapely figure. Joya liked statement jewelry and had selected the perfect pieces to complement her outfit. Sam said so. "You are WEARING that dress! Girl...you better watch out!"

She looks great...but Joya is an expert at putting up a good front when she wants to, Sam secretly thought.

Two beautiful, confident women who had the attention of many around them, completed their embrace and compliments of each other and took their seats to get ready for good food and even better conversation. Joya and Sam were the best friends and shared each other confidences. Just like her sister Mona always had her back, so did Sam. Sam and Mona were sometimes in competition with each other when it came to Joya. It made her uncomfortable sometimes, so Joya deliberately kept her sister and best friend apart as much as possible. Sometimes it was impossible – like at her wedding ceremony to Troy.

Never one to mince her words, Sam directly asked, "So, tell me what's going on with you since you dropped that most explosive bomb on Troy two weeks ago! Girl – I am still laughing at the look on his face when you took the rings back and chopped him down to size!"

Joya laughed with her friend as they clinked their glasses of mimosa to toast Joya's performance at the wedding. They both took a sip and set their glasses down. Joya had a lot to tell Sam but wanted to eat first. "Let's go up to the buffet. I'm starving."

"Right behind you, sister!"

Chapter 7

After the last bite of delicious smoked salmon with capers on her bagel, Joya took a sip of her second mimosa. She needed liquid courage to tell Sam the recent turn of events in her complicated life.

"I'm going on vacation in two weeks," she said waiting for Sam's response.

"Great! Where are we going?" Sam asked, always ready to travel, especially with her best friend.

Joya had to laugh. " 'WE' are not going anywhere! I'm not sure where we are going. David is planning everything." The bomb was dropped and duly exploded.

Sam banged her hand on the table and pushed back from the table scraping the wrought iron chair across the wooden deck. She did not realize how much noise she was making until people turned to see what was happening.

Joya gave her the look. Sam returned the look.

"Joya... You. Are. Going. To. Make. Me. Slap. You. In. Public!" she said emphasizing each word for full effect. "Look – I know that David definitely looked out for you and was very instrumental in preventing you from making one of the biggest mistakes of your life – marrying Troy, BUT – I CANNOT believe that you are going to take your little non-sexual affair with him to the next level! What about him being MARRIED don't you understand?!" she whispered loudly, leaning across the table.

Joya slightly slouched in her chair, put her hands together as if in prayer and looked out on the water. *How many times have I looked out on this same water? Sam is right, but I just don't want to be lonely.* Sam had been brutally honest, and Joya was bruised. She sat in silence, still looking at the water. A Delta flight was coming in for a landing. Another was taking off. Two planes passing each other in the air. Joya wondered about the people on those flights. Are there couples traveling together? Is anyone as on board as lonely as she? Has anyone been betrayed as she had been? Is there a man and woman sneaking away like she and David were planning to do?

Joya had to stop the pictures running through her imagination. Her thoughts combined with Sam's admonition, was destroying the relaxed Sunday afternoon mood that she'd started with earlier.

She was hurt, but chose her words carefully. "Sam – I hear what you are saying, but David is a good man. I think that he is ready to leave his wife. This trip might be his way of showing me that this is the first step towards that. They don't have a marriage anyway. Remember, she validated that herself."

"If he was such a 'good man', he wouldn't be CHEATING on his WIFE!" Sam snapped.

Joya snapped right back. "Mona has William! YOU don't seem interested in men! I don't intend to spend my life alone! It might be okay for you to lose yourself in your career, but NOT for ME!" Joya got up to leave, and then quickly decided against it. She knew that Sam only wanted the best for her. She did not want this or anything to destroy their friendship. But, she couldn't take back the words that had just come out of her mouth.

If Joya's words hurt Sam, she didn't show it, but she thought, *"This little light-skinned heffer is REALLY testing me! She has a lot of nerve!"*

In consideration of what Joya had just been through and not wanting to hurt her feelings, despite Joya's apparent disregard for Sam's feelings, Sam simply offered her best advice in that moment. "Just be careful."

Sam signaled for the check. She was ready to bring this meal with Joya to an end. They usually overstayed their welcome when they went out to eat, but she wasn't getting through to her friend. They needed to part ways before they both said something to put their friendship at risk. Plus, Sam was sensitive to the fact that Joya must still be hurting from the recent debacle with Troy and did not want to add salt to the wounds. She would have to say some extra prayers for her.

Joya sat across the table in silence while Sam paid the check. She considered Sam's admonishment and warnings.

But, ever the risk-taker, she had already decided to go for it with David.

Chapter 8

David sat at the upscale Black's Sports Bar & Grille with his best friend, Teddy. They had grown up together and had been friends since first grade. They often met on Sunday afternoons to watch sports together. It didn't matter the season; they would watch any sporting event. It made it easy for them since Teddy owned the sports bar. Teddy purchased the restaurant from the previous owner five years ago. David helped him to develop the pro forma and other supporting financial documents. He continued to function has the chief financial officer, part-time, for a nominal fee and free food and drink whenever he came in.

Since Teddy had a full staff and rarely ever worked at the restaurant, he was able to hang out with his buddy pretty much any time that they wanted. He had other profitable business ventures that were also generating income for him and was well-known as a fair business man and employer in the community.

He had spared no expense decorating the restaurant so that it would be appealing to both men and women that follow sports. Teddy wanted women to feel as comfortable watching sports there as the men. In keeping with the name, black was the predominant color of the table cloths, napkins and posh leather chairs for the bar and restaurant area.

To add flair, there were accents of white, with splashes of red throughout. The servers' uniforms consisted of black bottoms, white tops and red neckties for the men and the women. For special events, the staff would add a red or black fedora to their regular uniform. The customers loved it and sometimes would come in with their own red, black and white outfits.

Teddy took a sip of his beer. "What's been up, man? How're the kids doing?"

"It's all good. Kids are doing great. I'm getting ready to go on vacation in a couple of weeks." His trip with Joya was less than two weeks away; they were leaving on the following Saturday.

"Vacation? Wow! Are you taking the whole family? Or just you and Lynn?" Teddy asked, surprised to hear about David's travel plans, knowing his situation with Lynn.

"Come on, man. You know that Lynn and I are not going on vacation together," David sharply answered.

"Okay. Sorry. I was just asking! I thought things might have turned around for you two."

"Not in a million years." As David's closest confidante, Teddy knew about his situation with his wife, but David had only told Teddy a little bit about Joya. He needed to confide in him now and get his opinion.

"Do you remember Joya that I told you about?" He asked waiting for Teddy's confirmation that he remembered.

"Yeah. She's the lady that was in a bad deal with her fiancé? Whatever happened with that?" He asked curiously.

David brought Teddy up to speed on most of what had transpired with Joya and the pivotal role that he had played in her decision. Teddy listened without interrupting. He had two words in response to what David had just recanted for him: "Wow, man!" He thought for a moment. "That's deep. What's next for her? And you?"

"I care about her, man. After what she went through, I just want to scoop her up and take her away somewhere. Just us."

This was a lightbulb moment for Teddy. " Oh...I get it now. The vacation you are going on is with JOYA. Hmmmm..."

"What is 'hmmm' supposed to mean?" David asked, not expecting that response from Teddy.

"Hey – I get that you care for her, but you are still married. I also know that it isn't really a marriage, but you know how women can be. And men, for that matter, to be honest. The person that you THINK you don't want to be with always looks better with SOMEONE ELSE!"

David knew what Teddy meant, remembering Lynn's recent behavior, which he had not disclosed. It was way too embarrassing. "I hear you. But what am I supposed to do? Stop living and loving because my wife doesn't want a relationship with me?"

Teddy thought for a moment. "Love? So, you love Joya?"

David honestly responded, "I do love her. She's great. I know that she is the type of woman that I've always wanted to be with. She is smart, fun, beautiful; and the best part is that she is a good friend to me. Aside from you, she is the only person that I can share my confidence."

This is deep, Teddy realized. He adjusted himself in the bar chair, thinking about what to say next that would be helpful to his buddy.

"You deserve a relationship like that. As your best friend, I want that for you. But these things never end well. Are you prepared for how Lynn might react if she finds out? And what if Joya decides that she wants a true, full-time, committed relationship with you? I don't see how you would make it work with your responsibilities at home, with the kids and not to mention how much time you spend at your office."

"I spend time at work so that I'm NOT at home. Once the kids have everything they need, I'm out. I run errands or head to the office. It's the only way that I'm sure to have some peace. Lynn is a good mother – for the most part, but I think she purposely tries to push certain buttons with me."

Teddy grabbed a handful of bar mix. He munched on mini pretzels and peanuts while concentrating on what he had just heard. "I didn't realize it was that bad," Teddy said, genuinely concerned for his friend. "That can't be a good situation for anyone." *Especially the kids.* "So, why don't you leave?" he asked while giving David a manly shoulder squeeze. This was dangerous territory to tread, but he had to ask.

"I wish I could, man. But, I just can't." Avoiding eye contact, David took a sip of his beer and fixed his gaze to the game that was playing on the flat screen television above the bar.

Since he was already in the danger zone, Teddy wouldn't let it go. David very much needed a reality check – with himself, and he was going to give him a boost. *He wants the best of both worlds, but it doesn't work that way.*

"You can't? Or you won't?"

Chapter 9

Mona hit the button on her rearview mirror to close the garage door. She opened the door to her silver Mercedes Benz and swung her long, shapely legs to exit the car. She entered the rear foyer of her house and called out for William. She was surprised to see his car was in the garage.

"William! I'm home!"

"Hey, sweetie! I'm in the office." Mona followed the long hallway until she reached her office. William was busy removing very large pieces of art from the walls. Mona had asked him to do it only a few days ago. She loved that about him. She only had to ask him to do something once, and he was on it. He had left work early since it was Friday. He had already removed three pieces that had been carefully wrapped to protect the frame and glass. He was resting the final piece on the floor when Mona stepped up to him and kissed him 'hello.'

He put his arms around her waist and pulled her to him. He returned her kiss, gave her a hug, and then he asked, "How was your day?" He wasn't just asking as a formality; he genuinely wanted to know how Mona's day had been.

"It was good! I see that you were able to get off early again."

"Yes. The Senior Vice-Presidents know that I soon won't have this luxury once my new responsibilities officially kick in. They are giving me a lot of latitude and time to prepare for my new position." William was excited about his new position as Vice-President of International Business Development and what it also meant for his life with Mona. He had been in love with her almost from the beginning. He had spent the last ten years proving it to her.

He knew from observing her relationships with her family and with her friends that she was uniquely authentic, and he wanted to be the man that she chose to spend the rest of her life with. He hoped that the recent events with Joya would not weigh too heavily on Mona, and he suspected there was still something going on.

"Have you talked to you sister about our plans yet?" He didn't want to press. Nonetheless, he was cautiously curious.

"Not yet. We've talked almost every day since she spent the night here a couple of weeks ago, but she leaves for vacation tomorrow morning, so I didn't want to bring it up. I think it's best if we wait until she returns."

"That's cutting it kind of close, don't you think?" he asked wondering why Mona delayed sharing their good news with her sister.

"It might be, but I thought that she might be in a different mindset when she returns and will take the news a little better. I thought about it, and it was a toss-up." Mona held one hand up, palm up. "If I tell her before she leaves, and she might decide not to go and even though I don't agree with her choice of travel companions, I think the trip will be good for her." Then she flipped her other hand. "If I tell her when she comes back, which is now what I've decided to do, she might have a meltdown."

He kissed Mona's forehead. "Okay, babe. You know your sister better than anyone. So I trust your judgment. Where would you like to have dinner tonight?"

Joya better not mess this up for us. I've worked hard for this and waited a long time. William knew it was a selfish thought, but an honest one.

Chapter 10

Joya waited while David checked them into the island resort. She had never seen anything like it before, and she had done her share of traveling. It had been a full day of travel. David picked her up at seven a.m. that morning and took care of everything as he had promised. They enjoyed a champagne breakfast in the First Class cabin on the first leg of their journey from Washington National Airport, connecting in Miami; and then on to the Dominican Republic. Joya was enjoying all of David's attentiveness and was glad that she accepted the invitation to vacation with him.

The resort lobby reminded her of the open-air lobby in Exuma where she and Sam had gone before. That was a different time. Joya whispered a prayer of thanksgiving for what that trip had meant for her. The lobby of The Pegasus Seaside Resort that David selected was much grander with Roman columns, marble tiled wall-to-wall waterfalls, massive crystal vases of bird of paradise and an aquarium floor.

Joya relaxed on the sea foam green and gold chaise as she patiently waited for David to complete the check-in. He has his back to her as he talked to the resort staff. He was dressed in a white linen shirt with matching walking shorts.

He is so handsome. I like his style and how those pants hang off of his butt just right. Joya laughed at herself, tried to stop her thoughts, but she couldn't resist. David was looking good at just under six feet tall, built like a football player, skin the color of latte and a smile of slightly crooked teeth that illuminated the room. Joya noticed that he was handsome when she first met him, but it was his charisma that captured her attention.

She was still smiling when David interrupted her musing. He had completed the check-in and was walking towards her. "Penny for your thoughts?"

"My thoughts are worth more than a penny," she said jokingly. She did not want him to know what she was thinking. It could be risky. For both of them. David grabbed her hand and helped her to her feet. The bellman was standing nearby, ready to escort them to their suite.

Joya was not prepared for the lavish accommodations when the bellman opened the door to their suite. David had made good on his promise of separate bedrooms; Joya never doubted that he would.

The suite was larger than some apartments that Joya had seen in the U.S. The living room/dining room combination was open, decorated in sea-foam green, coral, and white. They had a corner unit with a wrap-around balcony that could be accessed from the dining room and from her bedroom.

Both bedrooms had king sized beds with full en-suite bathrooms. The seashell molded sinks were accented with matching seashell fixtures that poured water from gold toned mermaids. The white towels were fluffy, soft and appeared to be brand new.

Joya walked from her bedroom onto the balcony from her bedroom that faced the ocean. She closed her eyes and welcomed the sunshine and sea breeze. She was lost in the moment and didn't hear David come out to join her. He had tipped the bellman well, which was usual for him.

"So. What do you think?" he asked wanting very much to wrap his arms around Joya, but knowing he needed to remain cautious and respectful. As much as he wanted to, he knew that he should not cross into her personal space – just yet.

Joya turned to him, trying to control the emotion welling, not sure where it was even coming from. "David, this is so beautiful. I never imagined that we would be staying at a place like this..."

Not sure what she meant, but still careful, David questioned, "What do you mean?"

Joya sensed that she had offended David. "I'm sorry! I didn't mean it like that! I know that you would only do the best. I'm just overwhelmed by all of this. It's so beautiful. I've never stayed anywhere with an ocean view before." Hastily trying to change the mood, she put her hand on David's arm and pulled him slightly towards her. As they faced the ocean together, she urged. "Have you ever seen anything so beautiful?"

David turned, looked deeply into Joya's eyes and responded carefully, but honestly. "No. I haven't."

He wasn't referring to the ocean.

Chapter 11

Alise had left Joya two voicemails on her cell phone. She tried calling her on Saturday and Sunday, but her phone when directly to voicemail. She decided to wait until Monday morning and try her office.

"Good morning. J-Alexander Consulting. This is Pamela. How can I help you?" Joya's office manager answered. She was on the last bite of her sausage and egg biscuit when the phone rang. She knew that she needed to change her diet before her short, round body got even more out of control. She could no longer blame it on post-pregnancy weight since her youngest just turned twelve. Despite the extra pounds, she still turned heads with her flawless vanilla skin, bubbly personality and short, curly hair cut.

"Hi, Pamela – This is Alise Cook calling for Joya." She had called the office before and expected Pamela to recognize her. Alise moved to Dallas right after graduation from college. Friends since their freshmen year, she and Joya had maintained their friendship as much as possible considering the miles that separated them.   Initially, they made a pact to visit each other at least once a year, but work responsibilities had made it difficult for the past five years. Alise traveled internationally for the software company that paid her well, and she was on an aggressive career trajectory. She was determined to succeed, even if it meant sacrificing some of her personal relationships.

"Hi, Ms. Cook. Joya is away from the office. Can I give her a message for you?"

"When do you expect her?"

Super protective of her boss, Pamela didn't give an inch. Friend or otherwise. She only gave specific information about Joya's whereabouts to Mona and Sam. And even then, she was guarded. She took her job as Joya's assistant and office manager seriously. If it weren't for Joya, she and her children would probably be in a shelter, not sure where their next meal would come from.

None of your damn business. "I'd be happy to give her a message for you," she returned in her most professional voice while rolling her eyes to the telephone. She had learned to conceal her true feelings and control her tone on the telephone from the best: "Bosslady," as she affectionately called Joya.

Alise removed the phone from her ear and looked at it like she couldn't believe that Pamela was not answering her question.

You hood rat! You wouldn't even have a job if it weren't for Joya! She tapped her perfectly manicured nails on her desk to abate her anger. "Please tell her that I called, and I need her to call me back asap. It's important." Alise emphasized 'important.'

The More Things Change   Elle Nora

"Sure. No problem, Ms. Cook. I will give her the message. Is there anything else that I can do for you?" The question was posed more so to irritate Alise.

"No. There is nothing else. Thank you." Alise disconnected before Pamela could irritate her any further.

I really need to talk to Joya. I should have called her sooner...

Page | 43

Chapter 12

Joya and David spent a lazy Sunday on the beach reading, sleeping, and even having their meals served to them while they relaxed in the cabana. Joya liked being spoiled. It was a brand new experience for her. David had not crossed the line with her, but her feelings for him were escalating.

Sunday relaxation was exactly what they both needed, but they agreed to hit the ground and explore the island on Monday morning. David hired a private tour guide for a full day excursion of sightseeing, picnic on a private island and one of his and Joya's favorite activities: shopping. The concierge recommended the tour company as one of the best on the island, catering to an upscale clientele and specializing in customized tours.

The black Lincoln Town Car picked them up promptly at eight o'clock a.m. Their driver, Monty, jumped out of the car to greet them. He shook hands with David and tipped his hat to Joya, showing respect. He was short, stocky and did not have the features of the natives that worked at the resort.

"G'mornin', sir. Ma'am" he said with more of a European accent than the West Indian accent that Joya detected in the speech of most of the locals. He swiftly and expertly opened the back door of the car to let them in. Making sure that David and Joya were comfortably seated, he reviewed the itinerary with them, validating everything that David had requested for their day long excursion.

David and Joya sat close together and relaxed in the soft leather, eagerly anticipating the day. David took a chance and gently touched her hand. He smiled at Joya, silently communicating that he was happy to be with her. She sweetly returned the sentiment. Taking that as permission, he enveloped her hand in his and began to listen to Monty's recitation of the history of the island.

When they stopped at historic buildings, Monty escorted them inside, continuing his professional narration. David continued to hold Joya's hand while they walked with Monty through each building and while riding from one destination to the other in the Town Car .

"This tour has some special treats for you, and we are at the point of the first treat," Monty said as he maneuvered the car on a rocky, dirt road. Not knowing what to expect, Joya slid closer to the middle of the seat so that she could see through the front windshield. She was amazed to see they were approaching the cliffs that she had read about, but the brochure did not capture the beauty of what they were now seeing.

Monty parked the car away from the other tourists, jumped out and opened the door to let them exit. He opened the trunk of the car and produced two cups of ice cold rum punch, topped with nutmeg for David and Joya. Initially thinking it was too early to drink alcohol, it was as if Monty read her mind. He produced a plate of fresh pineapple and sliced banana nut bread.

David gave her a look of approval as they accepted the food and drink. This was tailgating at its best. While they enjoyed the mid-morning snack, Monty recited the history of the cliffs and instructed them to take their rum punch and walk around as closely as they could. He pointed out a path for them to walk with the instruction of where to start and end. He gave David a wink and they started their walk.

Holding Joya's hand, David led the way according to Monty's instruction. They started out by walking to the edge of the cliffs, observing centuries of rock etchings and formation. It was incredible to see the natural incisions and blending of colors. Joya thought, *Only God.*

David only managed to utter, "Wow!"

They walked around the cliff almost full circle until they came to a path that Monty had pointed out to them. Other tourists were also on the path, some groups returning and all seemed to be talking at once.

Joya heard one little boy say to his dad, "That was AWESOME!" Joya and David smiled at the child's excitement. She noticed that their shorts were wet. When she looked up, she immediately saw why. She was awestruck at the spectacular waterfall and natural pool nestled at the end of the path.

"Oh my," Joya whispered.

David squeezed her hand in agreement. Seeing that others were enjoying the rare pleasure of nature, he pulled Joya towards the pool. By the looks of it, it was only about four feet deep. Accepting the invitation, Joya followed David's lead and removed her shoes. They stepped into the warm water and walked a few feet to a natural boulder and took a seat, their feet still in the water.

At a loss for words, Joya sat with David in silence. He sat slightly behind her, his arm wrapped around her, holding her hand that rested in her lap. He was glad to be close to her and wished this moment could last forever. He didn't think of what his life was back home, only what he was feeling sitting next to Joya.

"You two look so delightful. May I take your picture?" The photographer wading towards them had come out of nowhere. Joya and David looked at each other. They silently agreed and nodded, giving the photographer permission. David put both arms around Joya, and she rested into his embrace.

The photographer took several shots, reviewed them on his camera pleased with his work. "You will be pleased, Mon. This is the look of true love," he smiled. "You can pick up your pictures in ten minutes at the gift shop at the top of the cliffs where you came in."

Chapter 13

Monty looked in the rear view mirror at the happy couple sitting so close in the backseat, obviously in love. After the cliffs, he drove them to the opposite end of the island where he laid a quilted blanket on a private beach for David and Joya. Their lunch, transported in his cooler, consisted of colossal shrimp salad on a bed of butter lettuce, Smoked Gouda cheese, and french banquette; dessert was champagne and chocolate dipped strawberries. *Americans like their champagne and chocolate strawberries*, he thought.

He was driving them to the final component of their excursion: shopping at the high-end strip mall on the island. Not everyone could afford such a shopping trip, Monty knew.

He noticed how he looked at her, but quickly brought his attention back to the road. He took the right-hand turn into the parking lot.

"We have arrived at the best shopping here on our island. Please enjoy and take your time."

He hopped out with his usual quickness and opened the door to let them out. *Nice guy*, Joya thought. David was out of the car and reaching for her hand to help her out.

David wanted to get souvenirs for his office staff. Joya helped him select an assortment of island treats that featured miniature rum cakes, coconut candies, candied pineapple and rich chocolates. David asked for her help selecting t-shirts for his children. She felt uneasy helping him select the items; it was a reminder of his real life - with his wife and family. David sensed her mood.

"What's wrong? Tired?"

"No. I'm good," Joya lied.

"Are you sure?" he asked touching her cheek.

"Yep." Eager to change the subject, she nudged him to cross the street to a jewelry store that had caught her eye.

"Welcome!" How can I help you folks today?" They were instantly greeted by the salesclerk, Verona, who was tall and dark with a ton of micro braid extensions and way too much make-up.

"Just browsing," Joya answered. She walked to the side of the store where the rings and necklaces were displayed. David walked towards the Rolex watches. The salesclerk hated when couples split up like that. She never knew who to help first, and she did not want to lose part of her commission to the other clerk on duty that might help.

Since women are the ones who usually shop the most, she decided to follow Joya, who had started looking at the canary diamonds. *Way out of my price range.* She moved to the chocolate diamonds. Verona sensed that Joya was a woman with unique taste. She invited her to look at the blue diamonds.

"Would you be interested in seeing our latest in blue diamonds? We just received this necklace and matching earrings." She gingerly lifted the necklace from the case and handed it to Joya.

"Oh wow! This is beautiful!" David turned his attention from the watches to see what excited Joya.

"Let me help you try it on." Joya turned so that Verona could place the necklace around her neck. The three carat blue diamond, surrounded by two carats of white diamonds, brilliantly sparkled as it hung from a fourteen carat white gold lace chain. It was perfect as if it was made especially for Joya. She looked in the mirror, delighted at how the necklace looked on her. She had never seen anything like it.

"Let's see how the earrings look on you," Verona suggested. She removed the earring from the case and started to clean the posts with an alcohol pad. She helped Joya remove her earrings and replace them with the blue and white diamond drop earrings, also set in white gold.

David saw how beautiful Joya looked in the jewelry, but she had already decided not to spend that much money. She thanked Verona and started to turn her attention to David's browsing of watches. She walked to the other side of the store to see exactly what had David's attention. Joya almost choked when she saw the price of the twenty-four carat gold Rolex that David wanted to try on. Verona was secretly doing cartwheels, thinking of the potential commission.

Joya was not totally surprised when, after trying on the watch, David decided to purchase it for himself. *He can afford it. He makes a lot of money.*

Thinking about the hefty commission that she'd just made, Verona graciously accepted the American Express Black Card from David. "Thank you, sir. I will wrap this up and be right back with your watch." They exchanged a glance between them. Verona had been selling jewelry to tourists for a long time and recognized the look from David.

David put his arm around Joya's waist and walked towards the crystal figurines set in a glass case towards the front of the store. He looked towards the doors and saw Monty leaning against the Town Car, looking into the store. Monty quickly turned away when he saw that David was looking at him but returned his attention back to him when he realized that he was signaling to him that they would be out of the store in a few minutes. Monty waved back that he understood.

"He's a nice guy," Joya said. "He is," David agreed. "I have to make sure that I give him a big tip for driving us around today."

Verona emerged from the back of the store and handed David his black card along with a black shopping bag, with black satin handles, and the name of the store embossed in gold.

"Thank you so much for your business. I hope that you will enjoy!" *I'm getting ready to enjoy leaving early after THAT commission!*

Monty smiled as they approached the car and held the door open for them. He reached for the shopping bags that David was carrying. David surrendered the bags and watched as Monty placed them in the trunk.

He held on to black bag from the Jewelry store.

Chapter 14

Monty looked both ways before safely steering the Town Car onto the main street that would lead back to the resort. The couple had resumed their seats in the back, sitting close as usual.

"I hope you folks had a good day. The shopping was good, yes?"

"Oh – Yeah! Shopping was REALLY good for a certain someone!" Joya snickered, giving David a playful nudge.

Monty glanced at them in the mirror.

"Hey!" David said playfully. "What is that supposed to mean?"

"For the first time that I can remember, I didn't buy anything! YOU did some damage back there!"

"Yes, I did some damage," he agreed as he pulled a black and gold box from the bag he had placed on the floor beside him. He handed the black satin box tied with a gold satin ribbon to Joya.

Beyond surprised, she hesitated before accepting the box from David. "David, what is this? When…"

"Open it."

Joya released the ribbon and lifted the hinged top. Her breath caught in her throat when she saw the blue diamond jewelry that she'd admired in the store. Monty was inconspicuously taking it all in.

Aware that Joya was overwhelmed by his gift, David lifted the necklace from the box and gently placed it around her neck. He reclaimed the box and snapped it shut, earrings still inside.

He put his arm around Joya, who still sat in silence looking at the extravagant gift that she had just been given. She held the pendant that hung from the chain around her neck. It was even more beautiful than it looked in the store.

"David – I don't know what to say. Thank you." For the first time, Joya initiated affection between them. She looked deeply into David's eyes and surrendered any apprehension she still carried about their relationship. She softly and assuredly kissed David's lips.

How long had he waited for this moment? Still encircled in his arm, he tightened his hug around Joya. *Finally.* It gave him a warm feeling that she was finally accepting his feelings for her. He hoped that she didn't think that the gift was a gesture to buy her affection. He bought it to make her happy. He just wanted to see Joya happy. And he wanted to be the one to bring her joy.

Monty watched the road ahead of him but didn't miss a beat of what was going on behind him. The couple continued to sit in silence, the woman resting comfortably against the man's muscular chest. He had not seen wedding rings on either of them, but the expensive gift that had just been presented did not get past him.

There were only a few minutes before they would reach the resort. Monty broke the silence with the question to David. "Sir, we are close to the resort. Is there anything else that I can do for you and the lady before we arrive?"

David whispered to Joya asking if she needed or wanted anything. Having her answer, he thanked Monty and said that they were good.

"You are most welcome. How much longer will you be visiting with us?"

"We leave in two days," David answered.

"I hope that you have enjoyed your day and continue to enjoy the rest of your time here. I'm sure that your family will be glad to see you return. You have children, no?" After spending the day together, Monty thought they would not mind the question. He noticed the look of discomfort on Joya's face.

David cleared his throat and removed his arm from around Joya's shoulders. She moved away from him and sat up straight in the backseat. Monty noticed the non-verbals. "I have two children. A boy and a girl," David replied reaching into his back pocket to retrieve his wallet.

Ahhh. Monty had been right in his assessment. The lady is uncomfortable at the mention of his children. This couple is not married. In love, maybe.

Monty brought the car to a stop in front of the resort. With his habitual quickness, he opened the rear door and swiftly proceeded to the rear to retrieve David's shopping bags from the trunk. David met Monty at the rear of the car and handed him a one hundred dollar bill folded in half.

"Oh, thank you, Sir! And my wife and four children thank you," he said slightly bowing to David. As he handed the shopping bags to David, he asked how he planned to get to the airport in two days. David explained that he would arrange a car with the concierge as they were leaving on the first flight at seven a.m.

Placing the tip in his pocket, "Sir, it would be my pleasure to drive you and the lady to the airport so that you do not need to worry about arranging for a car. I will pick you up at five thirty a.m. The airport is close so that will give ample time," he waited for David's answer.

"Sure. That will work. We will see you then. Thanks!" David said has he extended his free hand to shake hands with Monty, in appreciation for today and also to seal the deal for the ride to the airport.

Nice Guy - working hard for his family, David thought. He was glad to help.

Chapter 15

It was a bittersweet moment for Joya. She enjoyed her time away with David, but their tryst was coming to an end; they would be leaving the island paradise in the morning. She was lost in her thoughts as she sat at the dining room table looking out at the ocean. David had arranged for Butler Service to prepare an in suite candlelight dinner so that he and Joya could conclude their vacation – the right way.

They feasted on the finest in surf and turf served at the resort, prepared in the kitchen of their suite: filet mignon, topped with lobster, crab and shrimp in a light garlic cream sauce served with steamed snow peas. The Butler left after assuring that nothing else was needed from him. David topped Joya's champagne as they shared a dessert of fresh strawberries crowned with Amaretto whipped crème. Joya thought that it was more Amaretto than crème, but she was enjoying it.

Joya was buzzing from the combination of champagne and dessert, but she totally trusted David and knew that he would not cross the line with her. He had held her hand, and they had kissed on the lips a couple of times, but he had not made any moves that made her uncomfortable. They were going home, back to reality tomorrow, and Joya intended to enjoy the rest of the evening with David.

David wanted it to be a special evening for the two of them. He planned the special meal especially for them, carefully selecting the menu and the champagne. He didn't want the evening to end without being close to Joya, but he knew that he had to stay within his boundaries. Though, he had an idea that Joya might not oppose.

For the first time on the trip, he pulled out his cell phone. He quickly scrolled to the selection he had in mind and walked over to the flat screen television. He found the right cable and plugged it into his phone. Before Joya knew what he was doing, she heard the voice of Maxwell coming from the television, singing "Lifetime." David returned to the table, held his hand for Julia to join him. He guided her to the middle of the room, took her in his arms and led her in a slow dance.

This feels good, Joya thought. *Too good.* She wouldn't look at David. She looked down at the floor. They continued to sway to the smooth richness of Maxwell's voice; David released her hand so that he could put both arms around her. Joya placed her other hand around David's neck, opposite where her other hand already rested. She decided to relax into the moment.

David gently massaged her back as he continued to lead Joya on their impromptu dance floor. *That feels so good*; Joya was not resisting. Looking up at David, who had his vision fixed on her the entire time, she was captivated by the adoration he freely and willingly expressed with his gaze. Responsively, Joya touched his cheek, returning the affection.

Maybe it was the alcohol, maybe it was the music, or maybe it was the magic invisibly created between two people falling in love that brought their lips and bodies together in passion and desire. They held each other close, not dancing anymore, touching and exploring instead. David was in disbelief that his dream of holding Joya close and passionately kissing her was finally coming true.

Joya had not felt this way since Keith, but she was not thinking about him now, only how she felt in David's arms, his soft, sweet kisses and the enchantment that surrounded them.

How long have I waited? David thought as he held Joya close and continued to kiss her softly and sweetly. He was trying to control his passion, but it was tough. He had not held a woman in his arms like this in so long and had not really made love to a woman in what seemed like forever. He and Lynn only had sex as a matter of convenience which was easy since they lived in the same house, but those times were becoming far and few between. There was no passion; no emotion - just the physical release of pent up sexual lust when they both needed it. Sometimes David wondered if she was getting hers from another man.

Wanting more, David backed up to the sofa, Joya followed, their lips still connected. He sat down slowly; Joya followed easing down to straddle his lap. She could feel David's desire for her.

She unbuttoned his shirt, placing her hand inside. She felt the soft hair on his chest, and he trembled with an increased desire for her as he lifted her sundress. He stroked the soft skin on her legs, moving his way up to her firm hips. He heard her moan, which made him want her more. He caressed her hips through her lace panties, careful not to move too fast. He was still cautious, but not sure how much longer he could keep his desire at bay. Joya was resting firmly on his bulge, and he could feel her heat – heat that she had for him.

The next song on the playlist had started. Neither of them paid attention to exactly what the song was or who was singing it, but that did not prevent them from using it as a platform of soulful, sensual rhythm. They rocked with each other to the melody, David arching his pelvis in a carnal offering. Joya felt David's desire enlarge, and she was aware of her heat surging as their rhythmic pressure intensified. She definitely wanted what he was offering.

"Please, Joya," David moaned. "I want you so bad."

She saw the desire in his eyes matched his physical yearning. He appealed to Joya physically and emotionally. She responded with a kiss of passion that David longed for and hungrily accepted.

What am I doing? I can't do this! He is a married man! Joya heard the screaming in her head. She was falling in love with him, but she could not, would not make God angry by committing adultery.

She pushed his tongue from her mouth and released her lips from his. Still on his lap, she stroked his cheek, "David, I'm so sorry. I can't..." He stopped her.

"Joya, it's okay. I told you we would not do anything that you don't want to do." He removed his hand from under her dress and gently swung her off of his lap, but still holding her in his arms. He wasn't ready to let her go. She put her arms around him and laid her head on his chest.

Chapter 16

Joya tossed and turned in her bed thinking of David in the other bedroom and the magical, mystical evening they shared. She reminisced about his kisses, how the held each other close and how she was feeling about him. And for him. She had not fully recovered her earlier sensual desire for him.

Joya looked at the clock. It was one fifteen. She had not been asleep, and it would soon be time for them to get up and leave for the airport. *We will be back home tomorrow. What happens then? I don't want to go back to being lonely and alone. I'm falling in love with David, and I can tell that he loves me, too. He is a good man – the type of man that I've been dreaming of. WHY does he have to be married? WHY can't he just leave his wife and choose me? I can't lay here anymore...*

Joya got out of bed and walked into the kitchen to get some water. She noticed that David had left the door to his bedroom opened. She saw from the light that streamed in from the full moon that David also wasn't asleep. He had his back to the door and was rubbing his head; she could hear him breathing heavily.

Joya approached the room, slowly and quietly. She stood in the doorway admiring the muscles in David's arms and back, remembering how those arms felt around her and her hands on his back earlier.

Lost in his thoughts and fighting his own insomnia, David did not hear her approach but felt her petite body slide into bed behind him, wrapping her arms around him.

He exhaled, holding her hand that rested on his chest. "Joya-" he started to turn over. She stopped him. "Good night, my love," she said kissing his back, wrapping her legs in his and tightening her embrace.

David relaxed. Joya rested her head on his back and felt a sense of calm.

Their exclusive magic had reappeared, casting the spell of much needed sleep for the both of them.

Chapter 17

Joya stood near the entrance of the resort lobby while David checked them out and took care of the bill. She saw Monty drive up in the Town Car, right on time as he'd promised. He pulled right up to the entrance where Joya stood with their luggage.

"Good morning, miss," he tipped his hat to Joya. David turned when he heard Monty's voice. Waving, he informed Monty, already loading the luggage in the trunk, that he was finishing up. "No problem! Take your time." He opened the door to let Joya inside.

With his passengers comfortably settled in, Monty glanced at them in the rearview mirror while expertly navigating the car in the early morning darkness. David held Joya's hand, just as he had the entire trip two days before, but they seem closer today. "I hope you enjoyed your visit," Monty started making eye contact with David.

"We did. We had an unforgettable time," David said squeezing Joya's hand. She looked at him with the smile that made his heart melt. He touched the blue diamond necklace that she wore around her neck. It matched her lightweight denim maxi dress perfectly, and he was glad that he purchased the jewelry for her. Monty also noticed that she was wearing the jewelry that the man had bought for her the last time they rode in his car.

David whispered something in Joya's ear, then kissed her on the cheek. She said something to him that Monty could not hear. He steered the car off of the main road onto a dirt road. David and Joya didn't notice until the car hit a bump in the road that startled them.

"Whoa!" David yelled, turning his attention away from Joya. "Did you have a flat tire?" he asked Monty. He looked up noticing that they were no longer on the main thoroughfare.

"No flat tire. Give me your cell phones. Both of you," Monty turned pointing a small pistol at them.

Chapter 18

Joya screamed. David pushed Monty's hand. "Stop playing, man. And put that thing away."

Monty had turned sinister. "You think I'm playing? If you don't give me your phones right now, I will shoot you both and leave you here. AFTER I take all of your money, your jewelry, AND your clothes." Flabbergasted, but not taking a chance with their lives, David still holding Joya's hand, reached into his pocket with his free hand and surrendered his phone to Monty. Joya reached into her purse for her phone and handed it to Monty.

He placed their phones into a black leather man purse. "Now, give me your tickets, passports, and your driver's licenses." They once again obeyed, Joya was praying that a car would pass soon, and David was fuming, wanting badly to kick Monty's little short ass.

"Man, what is this?! Why are you doing this?" David demanded.

Monty ignored David's questions. "Take out your wallet," he said pointing the gun at David. "Yours too," he turned to Joya.

"If you wanted money, you should have just asked. You don't have to threaten us with that gun. Put it away," he urged once again.

"Shut up! Give me all of the money from your wallets! And your BLACK Amex!" he shouted. Joya didn't have much cash, but she gave him all that she had in her wallet. David gave up his black American Express and about eight hundred dollars in cash. He was fuming because he had planned to pay Monty well for the trip to the airport.

He smiled at Joya. "The necklace. And the earrings. NOW!" he yelled at her. Joya hesitated, but she didn't flinch.

David lost it. "Man, I will fu—" He was stopped before he could finish spitting the words out of his mouth. Joya had never seen David this angry. But, she also had never been robbed at gunpoint with him before.

Monty raised up, reached across the seat and put the gun to David's head. "Oh yeah? Really? I think you better just do what I say before I pull the trigger. Then this little slim goodie will have to explain why I shot you to YOUR WIFE," he spat.

How does he know that?! Oh my God! Joya screamed inside as she touched David's arm. "David – stop!" she pleaded with him as she removed the necklace and handed it to Monty. Before he could ask again, she removed the earrings and handed them over. She would do anything to prevent them from being murdered.

Chapter 19

"Now get out of the car. This time, you open your own door." Monty spat at David as he opened his door with his free hand and backed out of the car, still holding the gun on his passengers.

Joya was trembling and praying silently. Once they were standing outside of the car, Monty opened the trunk and placed Joya's jewelry in a black plastic bag. He told David to open up his carry on.

"What for? You going to shake me down for my shaving cream now?" David asked sarcastically.

Joya cringed. *What about having a gun pointed at him doesn't he understand?*

"No, smart guy. You are gonna give me that gold Rolex that you bought in town the other day. Yeah, I saw you buy it. You aren't wearing it, so I know that you packed it in your carry on. Give it to me."

He's done this before, David realized and it made him angrier. *I can't believe that I'm being robbed by his little punk ass!* He reached into the black leather carry-on and removed the watch, still in the case. He handed it to Monty. "That's it. We have nothing else to give you. Now, what?"

Directly answering David's question, "Now, you get in the front seat, and the lady gets in the back, and I'm going to drive you to the airport. If you try anything, I will shoot you both."

Chapter 20

Thank you, God. Joya could see the airport in the distance in the darkness now parting to the morning dusk. *Someone will help us once we get inside.*

"This is what's going to happen," Monty said, driving with one hand, gun pointed at David with the other. "I'm going to escort you all the way through customs and security, and I will keep your passports and tickets until it is time for you to board. Don't even think of saying anything to anyone because without your passports, you will be detained on our little island. If you don't follow my lead all the way through, I will run like hell with your i.d. And your passports. And your tickets. I know all of the hiding places in this airport and on this island. If, for some reason, they find me and arrest me, they will hold all of your stuff in evidence – indefinitely.

Try going to the U.S. Consulate without your identification and see how far you would get. You might as well say goodbye to ever seeing your families again."

THIS little son-of-a-bitch! David wanted to grab the gun from him and beat him with it, but he knew that he couldn't risk Joya's life. Or his own. *He has a little racket going; probably has people inside the airport working with him.*

Monty parked the car across from the entrance to the airport where the limos and taxis were allowed to park when they were transporting VIPs, which was the case for him today.

He told David to get out of the car first. Then Joya. Then he got out, discreetly holding the gun on Joya. He had released the trunk and instructed David to pull out their luggage. He reminded them once more what would happen if they tried anything. He placed their travel documents and passports in the inside breast pocket of his blazer. He placed the gun in a tool box in the trunk.

"Get that frown off of your face," he said to David as he signaled for a Porter to help them with their luggage.

Chapter 21

The Porter led the way with David and Joya's luggage on his cart; Monty brought up the rear of the group, carefully watching his passengers. He had transformed back to the tour guide that he had been when they first met him, pleasantly and professionally presenting their tickets and passports to the ticket agent, who checked their bags and handed their claim checks to Monty.

Monty thanked her, then led David and Joya to the Customs area.

Surely, we can get someone's attention here, Joya thought.

Monty spoke to the one security guard with authority. "VIPs coming through," he said flashing some type of credential and Joya and David's tickets. The guard removed the barricade from the priority lane to let them through. Monty stepped aside so that Joya and David could go through ahead of him. He was right on David's heels, whispering to him, "When you get to the window, step aside and let me take over."

David gently gripped Joya's arm to move her aside when they arrived before the customs agent. Monty had their carry-on bags and their passports. He stepped to the window and said something to the agent in a language that neither David nor Joya understood. The agent never spoke to them, looking at them sideways, but quickly stamped their passports and handed them back to Monty.

Monty nudged them through to the inspection area. All three of them walked through the metal detectors, passing without incident and picked up their bags on the other side. There were only two departure gates, and Joya exhaled when she saw that a plane was outside on the tarmac parked at the gate they would be departing from. She could not wait for this nightmare to be over. She was worried about David. She could tell that he was angry; he was perspiring, and the veins on the side of his head looked like they were going to explode.

"Good job," Monty taunted. "Can I get you anything? Water? Soda?"

"Seriously?" David sneered. Joya stroked his back. "Let it go. We'll be boarding in a few minutes." Since they were traveling in the First Class cabin, they would be allowed to pre-board, which was scheduled to occur in less than fifteen minutes. As much as she detested Monty and what he was doing to them, they would soon be free of him. She had to keep David calm.

Even Joya's touch didn't calm him. *I cannot believe this! If Joya wasn't with me, I would kick his ass!* David declined Joya's invitation to sit down, so she continued to stand next to him, never leaving his side.

It seemed like the longest fifteen minutes of their lives. As soon as the announcement was being made for first class passengers to board, Monty reached into his jacket pocket, retrieving their cell phones and travel documents he had confiscated earlier.

David snatched the documents. "You little bitch!" he spat at Monty, but careful not to draw attention. They were too close to being free from the callous thief.

"It has been my pleasure to serve you. Have a safe trip." Monty said as he motioned them towards the ticket agent waiting to let them board.

Chapter 22

David slammed their bags overhead and fell into his seat. Joya was already seated, still going over the previous events in her mind. *Did that just happen?* When she comprehended the danger that they had been in, she breathed a prayer of thanksgiving for herself and David. God had saved them.

She was aware that David was still fuming, but she concentrated on praying. She was facing the window, eyes still closed when she felt David put his arm around her. She started to cry and would not turn away from the window. All the terror of the morning overflowed from Joya in her soundless tears.

"Joya – look at me. Are you okay?" Joya nodded without turning.

The head flight attendant noticed Joya and David. She carefully approached them. "Can I get you two anything?"

"Yes! How about the police?" David said too harshly and quickly apologized. He knew it would not do any good to explain to her what had just happened. He would have to deal with it when he returned to the states. In the interim, he ordered a stiff drink from the flight attendant and turned on his cell phone that Monty had returned to him. He opened up his AMEX app and froze his black card. *Now, Bitch! Try and charge something!* He reviewed his recent transactions, and nothing had been charged so far. He received confirmation of his request to freeze the account.

With that taken care of, he returned his attention to Joya. He reached for her hand. "Let me get you something to drink. Would you like some water? Or Tea? Joya, I'm so sorry about what happened..."

Not wanting him to see the ugly crying face, she reached into her purse for a tissue. Once she composed herself, she turned to him. While she was praying, she had also beat herself up for being in the situation in the first place; being away with a married man, a man with a family although they were truly falling in love. They had shared an enchanted week together, but it wasn't right. She knew that it wasn't his fault, but why else would a fairy tale end way that this one had?

She looked into his eyes and revealed her thoughts, choking the words, "I guess God really don't like ugly."

Chapter 23

Joya couldn't sleep; too many things swirling in her head. Instead of tossing and turning, she turned on the light on her nightstand and reached for the notepad and pen she kept there. She started to make a list of things she needed to do tomorrow, which was really today since it was already after midnight. She wrote each thought as it came:

1. Call Mona: *I promised that I would call her when I returned.*
2. Call Alise: *she left me two voicemails; what's up with her?*
3. Call Naya for a hair appointment: *I really need to get my hair done!*
4. Call Sam: *she will NOT believe what happened!*
5. Got to the grocery store: *need food.*
6. Go to the Wine Shop: *need wine – bad!*
7. Get a new life! *THIS one ain't working!*

She replaced the pad and pen but kept the light on knowing that she would not be able to sleep. She looked at the clock: twelve forty. Maybe Alise would still be up since she was in the central time zone and one hour behind. She picked up her cell phone, scrolled to find the voice mail from her and selected 'call back.' Alise answered on the second ring. *Good, she is still up.*

"Hey girlfriend," she answered so glad to hear from Joya. She immediately answered when she saw her picture display on her caller id. "What are you doing still awake after midnight?"

"Girl, you would not believe it if I told you!" she said testing the waters with Alise. They were the best of friends, but it was hard to detect her mood sometimes, however Joya thought that her answering the phone was a good sign. She recounted the entire saga of the storybook trip with David that had a ghastly ending. Alise always enjoyed Joya's stories, and she hung on her every word. If Joya had not told her the events of the vacation herself, she would not have believed what she was hearing.

"Oh my God!" she said. "I cannot believe that you were robbed! But, the good news is that you are both okay. What happens now – are you and David filing a police report?"

"I haven't talked to him since he dropped me off yesterday, but I think he plans to. I don't think there is much that can be done, but I'll keep you posted." Remembering that Alise had left her two voice mail messages, she tossed the ball into her court. "So, enough about my craziness. What's going on with you?"

Alise enjoyed Joya's story so much, she had gotten lost in it and forgot her own reality – just for a moment. She took a deep breath and then exhaled.

"I received some not-so-good news a couple of weeks ago."

Oh no! Joya held her breath and braced herself. She anticipated what was coming and was already in silent prayer for her girlfriend. She pictured her beautiful friend on the other end of the line with her flawless brown skin, bright smile, and attractive figure. Alise continued, "I went to the doctor last month for a routine check-up. She filled out a referral for me to have my annual mammogram; again routine. I thought nothing of it until the tech started to frown her face during the test. I don't know why they do that. We are the ones getting our boobs pulled, twisted and smashed and THEY have the nerve to be frowned up. But anyway, she said that she wanted to do a sonogram, which I thought was strange. Long story short: after several more tests, biopsies and second and third opinions, it is the dreaded diagnosis that none of us want to hear." She refused to say the word, but Joya already knew. "My surgery is scheduled for next week," finished with delivering her bad news once again, she waited for Joya's response.

Alise felt that delivering the news of her diagnosis was, in some ways, worse than the actual diagnosis. She had already told her family and closest friends, with Joya being the last one, because she hadn't been able to reach her. Her mother was her constant strength, but some of her girlfriends had broken down and made her feel worse. Despite the unexpected and unnerving reactions she received, she resolved to be strong and to fight for her life. Up to this point, she had not had any close family, or friends for that matter, to receive "the diagnosis."

She didn't receive the diagnosis from her doctor as a death sentence. She immediately went into research mode, gathering as much information as possible in order to make a qualified decision and to choose competent doctors. She would need major surgery to remove the disease. Based on everything that she read, and doctors that she consulted, she was confident that she made the right decision for her specific care plan.

Drawing on her inner strength, and praying for the right words, Joya took a silent, but deep breath. "It sounds like you are comfortable with your doctors and everything they've told you. I'm sorry that you have to go through this, but you won't go through it alone. I'll come out to help you through your surgery."

"No! I don't want any company! My friends here will help me!"

Company? Taken aback, Joya had no idea where that came from, and her feelings were bruised. *This is not about me*, she thought. *I'm not going out there to hang out, I just wanted to help.*

"Ok. I understand. Just give one of your friends my cell number so that they can keep me updated on everything next week. I'll be praying for you on this end and if you need me to do anything, please just let me know."

   Alise agreed to connect Joya with the survivor/mentor that was assigned to her. Knowing that she had probably hurt Joya's feelings, she said she had another call coming in. It was not her intention to say what she had, but she felt that no one could really empathize. She was the one who have been given the diagnosis. *I should have a few trump cards right now with my family and friends. They should understand...*

Chapter 24

It was a sleepless night for Joya replacing thoughts of the trip with David with concern and repeated prayers for Alise. She put an end to the tossing and turning, rising with the sun. Remembering the list she had made the night before, she checked off the item to call Alise. Today, she would go to the grocery store, call Naya to make her hair appointment and call Mona. *Maybe I'll go over instead,* she thought looking forward to seeing her sister. She would call Mona and ask if she could stop by after work, though she was not planning to tell her about the ghastly events of her trip.

Since it was Joya's last day of vacation before returning to work on Monday, she would hit the grocery store before the Friday evening rush. That would give her time also to check in with Naya for an appointment to get her hair done, and then hopefully see Mona afterward.

Fridays always put Joya in a better mood, despite what might be going on and today was no exception. Regardless of the lack of sleep, she showered, dressed enjoyed a cup of green tea and then took off to run a few errands before the major task of grocery shopping, which she didn't particularly like. Joya thought she could be so much more productive with the time she spent at the grocery store, but she also did not like grocery delivery. She preferred to select her own produce, which made up most of her groceries.

She called Naya from the car and made her hair appointment, gassed up the car, picked up her dry cleaning and completed her grocery shopping all before noon. Once she had a time from Naya – she didn't have an opening today, but one in the morning – she called and asked Mona if she could stop by after work. Mona agreed, also looking forward to seeing her sister.

She would let William know that Joya was coming over.

Chapter 25

Mona greeted Joya at the front door with an adoring hug, so glad that Joya was back from her vacation. "Look at you all tanned and beautiful!" she lovingly exclaimed to her sister. *She must have gotten some while she was away – she has that glow,* Mona smiled at the thought. Joya was tanned from her days with David relaxing on the beach and touring the island. She looked so much better than the last time Mona saw her after the nightmare had drained Joya of the little color she had and produced dark circles around her eyes. She had no idea how tragic Joya's trip had turned or the bad news that she received about her girlfriend upon her return.

Leading Joya to the kitchen, she asked, "Did you have a good time? How did you like the D.R.?"

"It was great," Joya answered referring to the better part of the trip. She was not going to subject herself to Mona's admonishment by revealing the truth of how her trip with David had ended. Eager to change the subject, "So what have you and William been up to?" she asked. Something seemed different to Joya about the atmosphere in Mona's home, but she wasn't quite sure what it was.

She's not telling me something. Mona was always able to read Joya. Sometimes she would press her and other times she would back off. Not sure how she should proceed – or not with Joya, the decision was made for her when she heard William come in through the rear foyer door making his way to the kitchen where she and Joya sat.

William knew that Joya would be there – Mona told him. He was glad to hear it. "Hey, ladies. Joya – look at you! You look great!" He meant it and was hoping that Joya's recovery from her recent events would mean that Mona would also feel better. "Hey sweetie," he kissed Mona on the cheek.

"Hi, William. How's everything at work?" Joya asked.

Glad you asked, William thought, hoping that Mona would proceed with talking to Joya as they agreed.

"It's going well," he responded. "Very well," he looked at Mona. "Anyone want to join me for a glass of wine?"

"Sure," Joya and Mona replied in unison.

William uncorked a bottle of Red Zinfandel that he brought in with him while Mona placed three wine glasses on the granite counter for them. William poured a sample into his glass, did the ceremonious sniff, swirl, and taste. Satisfied, he poured a glass for each of the ladies, and then himself. Raising his glass, "I'd like to propose a toast. To the woman that I love and our exciting future together."

Mona cringed but quickly recovered. *I wish he hadn't said that.*

Huh? Something I don't know? Joya wondered. She clinked glasses with Mona and William, not saying anything. Mona sipped her wine, eyeballing William; he returned the gaze. The silence between the three of them was profoundly awkward.

Joya noticed the glances between Mona and William; and decided to break the silence. "So are you two finally getting married?" she asked getting right to the point. She was not really in the mood to dance around with them. William brought it up, so they should be totally forthcoming instead of peeping at each other over their wine glasses like she wouldn't notice. She took a second sip of her wine while she waited for one of them to answer. *Anytime today!*

Another silent exchange before Mona finally answered, "Yes. We are getting married. It will be a private ceremony, but we hope that you will be there?"

"Oh my God! Of course, I will be there! How could I NOT be there?" Joya was so happy for Mona. And William. She wondered when they had made the decision and set the date. She had been lost in her own drama and hoped that didn't spoil Mona's plans. She had so many questions. "Just tell me when and where!" Joya screamed which prompted another glance between Mona and William.

WHAT is going on with them? Joya was on an emotional rollercoaster with these two – happy for the news of their nuptials, but tired of the secret looks. It was making her more uncomfortable. She looked at them waiting for an answer.

Mona decided not to delay sharing the news with Joya any longer. She and William had waited as long as they could...but it was time. Not really a drinker, she was already starting to feel the wine after only two sips. She set her glass down, not planning to drink any more of it; William would finish it.

Looking at Joya, "You remember William's promotion right before you left for vacation?" she asked. Joya nodded her head, sipping her wine, almost to the end of what William had poured into her glass. "Well, it's a REALLY BIG promotion. William is going to be in charge of the International Sales Division," she said proud of her man.

"That's great!" Joya said sincerely happy for William's promotion and what it would mean for them. *Mona deserves to be happy – especially with a man like William that can provide for her and take care of her.*

"Thank you! We're so excited," Mona openly expressed to her sister. William was glad that she was finally sharing her excitement. It was long overdue. Mona accepted Joya's excitement as confirmation; she continued, "We are getting married in Paris." She held her breath, waiting for Joya's reaction. She didn't have to wait long. Joya jumped from the bar chair and wrapped her arms around Mona. "Paris! Mona – you have always wanted to go to Paris. This is so great! It will be beautiful! YOU will be beautiful!" She was so thrilled for her sister, she almost forgot that William was an essential element in this major event. With one arm still around Mona, she reached for William forming a group hug.

The pieces were fitting together in Joya's mind. "So, William – Paris must be in your international territory? Is that why you two decided to get married there?"

Again – I'm glad you asked. "That's part of it. Actually, I will be the Vice-President in charge of the Paris sales team. Mona and I will be living there."

Chapter 26

Joya broke the circle that she initiated and released her hug. She picked up her glass and drained what was left of the wine. It wasn't enough. She picked up Mona's glass, which had been barely touched and guzzled it until the glass was empty. She set it on the counter, making an audible clanking sound that matched the sound of her heartbreak. As happy as she was for Mona, she was not prepared for her to move to another country. With Delia and Louis gone, she would not have close family around. Yes, Mona deserved to live her life and fulfill her dreams, but Joya depended on her and was already feeling her absence.

It occurred to her then what was different about the atmosphere in Mona's home. She had already begun to pack. Joya noticed that some of the artwork that had once hung in the rear and front foyers were absent from the walls. Composing herself somewhat, she offered an apology. "I apologize. It's just a shock. I wasn't expecting to hear that you are moving so far away." She said that more for William's benefit; she would have to talk to Mona honestly and privately later. "When are you moving?"

Disappointed but not surprised by Joya's reaction, Mona informed her that the relocation would occur within the next month and the wedding one month after that. It was happening so fast because of William's promotion and the need for him to take his position at the Paris location for which he would have responsibility for the completion of a new office there. They would need to be there for three to five years, and she was not planning to live with a man she was not married to. And it wouldn't make sense for them to live separately especially since they planned to be married. She could live together for a month – because they were planning to be married, but that was her limit.

Joya had to wonder if the relocation was William's strategy to force Mona's hand in marriage to him. He had wanted to marry her almost from the beginning, but Mona was in no hurry. At one point, she had even indicated that there was no need for them to get married. William already had a child from a previous marriage and Mona had decided that she didn't want children.

Joya stopped the thoughts knowing that she had no right to critique Mona and William's decisions. She, herself, had not made the best choices when it came to the men she had chosen. She counted David in that category.

Maybe if I wasn't so caught up starring in my own soap opera drama, Mona would have told me her good news sooner. I still don't want her to move away, but I have to be happy for her. She has ALWAYS been with me through all of my craziness. And how many times has she rescued our relatives and her friends? She deserves to be happy with William. And she has always dreamed of going to Paris – now she can live there! No matter what was happening in Joya's life, having Mona close by gave her a feeling of strength and composure and mutual reliance.

Mona repeated that she and William only had two months to make everything happen with the move to Paris and their nuptials. She appealed to Joya for her help and support to help make it happen.

"Of course," Joya assured her sister. "I will do whatever you need me to do. It looks like you already started packing," she said looking around.

"We have, but there's plenty left to do," Mona smiled. "I hope you can come to Paris the week of the wedding to help me with the final details? And be my maid of honor?" she waited for Joya's answer.

Joya hugged Mona again. "You know that I will. Maybe I can come for two weeks," Joya offered, seeing it as an opportunity to escape her own crazy life.

Chapter 27

Joya's emotions were all over the place as she drove home. She was excited for her sister, but she would miss her so much; she was her rock in so many ways. She would help her with the relocation and wedding, because she loved her and wanted to see her dreams fulfilled. Mona had a right to accept her blessings. *God has truly blessed Mona,* Joya thought as she turned the corner to approach her street. She was surprised to see his car parked in front of her house. *What is he doing here?*

David got out of his car when he saw Joya approach in his rearview mirror. He had just arrived. *Perfect timing*, he thought. Irritable, Joya pushed the button to open her garage door. *I can't believe he just showed up here without calling*, she thought as she scrolled through her phone to make sure that she had not missed his calls. There were no calls from him. He met her in the garage as she stepped out of her BMW.

"Hey," he said sweetly as he greeted her with a bouquet of red roses mixed with day lilies. "Hey," Joya returned the greeting. "What's this?" she asked not accepting the flowers.

"Just because," he said, pulling her into his arms, kissing her cheek. As much as she wanted to resist, Joya melted into his embrace, accepting his kiss and the bouquet. She wrapped her arms around him in a loving embrace, not sure where it was coming from since she had not fully recovered from beating herself up for taking the trip with him and their lives being at risk. She had prayed for forgiveness so many times, she sounded like a broken record to herself. Maybe she needed someone to lean on now that Mona was leaving. She led David by the hand inside her home.

David stood at the kitchen island while Joya put the flowers in a crystal vase she had filled with water. "I'm sorry for coming over without calling you, but I just really wanted to see you and was afraid that you would not answer my calls or just refuse to see me," he said waiting for her answer.

You got that right! Joya didn't answer, creating an awkward silence that made them both uncomfortable. He had planned to wait until later, but decided to inform Joya about what he discovered. Maybe, it would make her feel better.

"I found someone to help me with that 'situation' that happened to us," he reported avoided using the actual word 'robbery' as he knew it would upset Joya. He wanted her to know that he was taking care of the issue, but treading carefully so as not to trigger her feelings of remorse. Her words and actions on their return trip from the D.R. had gravely concerned him. The time and passion they'd shared had drawn them closer, which was what he had prayed for. If only he had not trusted Monty to take them to the airport...

Interested, Joya questioned, "Really? How so?"

Glad that the silence had been broken, David cautiously continued, "Long story short: I contacted a lawyer here who has connections with an international law enforcement council. They found out that Monty was a substitute driver for the tour company that I hired to drive us around. He has done this type of thing before - as I suspected - on other Caribbean islands and left the D.R. that same day on a flight not too long after we left. He tried to use my AMEX to charge his ticket, but I had already frozen it. They found the car abandoned in the parking lot. He is long gone, but I have people working on getting your jewelry back. He won't get away with it. I'm thinking the other tourists that he robbed were just glad to get back home alive and let it go. He is not getting away with it this time."

Joya took a deep breath, "David, thanks, but I don't want the jewelry back. I'm just glad that we are back safely. He didn't keep our identification, so he probably won't do anything to us here in the states. He is such a scumbag! Ugh!"

"That's why I won't let him get away with it!" David's male ego was determined not to let it go.

Again, an awkward silence. David joined Joya on the other side of the kitchen island where she stood, arms crossed staring at the flowers she had just placed in the vase. He took her into his arms, and she let it all go. She wasn't even sure why she was crying. He silently wiped her tears, feeling his heart breaking with each teardrop. He knew he was the cause of her tears and all he wanted to do was to make her happy. To protect her. And to make her his.

"Joya-sweetheart, I'm so sorry. I don't want to cause you any pain."

"It's not just this, David. My sister is leaving the country...one of my best friends has cancer...there's just so much going on..."

"Wow. That's a lot...but, I'm here for you. Whatever you need...have you eaten? Let's me take you to dinner." He knew just the place to cheer Joya.

"I'm not hungry. I don't feel like going out."

"Okay. Then I will go out and bring something back for us, and we can eat here?"

"Thanks," she said breaking their embrace. "I just need some time. I have an early appointment in the morning. I'll call you tomorrow afternoon. Maybe we can get together tomorrow?" she asked.

Preparing to leave, he offered, "Whatever you need, baby," tenderly kissing her lips. *Goodnight – for now.*

Chapter 28

Joya always looked forward to seeing Naya. It was more than a hair appointment for her. It was an opportunity to be pampered and to literally let her hair down and engage in honest dialogue. Although Naya was considerably younger in years, Joya recognized the "old soul" in her and appreciated her wise and candid counsel as well as her inner and outward beauty. Not only was she a talented hair stylist, she was a gifted music artist and vocalist with natural born talent. She also possessed the organic exquisiteness to be a model, always displaying her own unique style of dress. Joya couldn't remember seeing her with the same hairstyle twice in a row; today she strutted a full textured, curly afro that only she could pull off.

Naya admired Joya for her accomplishments and tenacity through the tough times. She often thought that other women she knew could benefit from taking a page from Joya's book of life.

Mutually glad to see each other, they hugged before Naya led Joya to the shampoo area. Her assistant usually shampooed her customers, but Naya always made a point to shampoo Joya herself. It gave them more 'sister-friend' time together. She attended Joya's "wedding" and knew the emotional roller coaster she was on right now, hence giving her an extended scalp massage. Joya rested in Naya's magical hands and was almost asleep when she heard her say, "Sit up for me." Naya was done with the shampoo, conditioning, scalp massage and rinse.

"Thanks, girl. I really needed that," she said lifting her head from the shampoo bowl. She followed Naya to her chair in the styling area. After making sure that she was comfortably seated, Naya inquired, "So, what's been going on? Are you doing okay?" She was genuinely concerned about Joya, especially after everything that happened with Troy. She had a lot to catch up on.

Joya took a deep breath and then exhaled. "I thought I was until a few days ago," Joya answered honestly. She brought Naya up-to-date on everything that had transpired with her trip with David and hearing about Alise's illness and Mona's wedding and relocation plans.

Naya was always even-tempered, never displaying upset or shock at what she heard from her customers. But, Joya was more than a customer; they had become friends and confidantes. While she listened to Joya, her heart went out to her as she thought, *"Wow. She just can't get a break. She is such a good friend to those she cares about, and she deserves a man who will love her and appreciate the strong-willed woman that she is. She has so much to offer..."* She was unsure which issue she should respond to first. Mulling it over for a few seconds, she decided to address the subject of Mona's relocation. "So, it sounds like you are happy for your sister, but you don't like the part of her moving so far away?"

Always so perceptive. "Yes, that's it. I know that she deserves to be happy, and she has always wanted to go to Paris; now she has the opportunity to live there. Even if it's only for five years, it will seem like forever to me."

"You will miss her – she's your sister and you two have always been close. You can Skype with her often, and you can always visit. I'm sure that her husband will also have to come back here for meetings, and if that is the case, I'm sure that Mona will come with him." Joya had not thought of that. Not waiting for Joya's response and skipping to the next topic, "I'm sorry to hear about your friend. I'm going to pray for her. It seems like this disease is happening more and more. I think there is something in our food and water making us sick. You wouldn't believe how many of my customers are undergoing chemotherapy treatments right now. I usually do their hair in the back to give them privacy. They don't want anyone to see their baldness, but I like to keep their scalp healthy with regular shampoo and moisturizing treatments." Naya had created her own line of hair and skin products from natural ingredients of Shea and essential oils.

Naya is such a gem – always willing to help her sister-friends however she can. I know the ladies that are going through their healing journeys appreciate

*what she is doing for them. She deserves a special
blessing,* Joya said a silent prayer for Naya.

"I agree. It's scary, and I want to help Alise, but
she doesn't seem to want my help. So, I'll just
continue to pray for her and be here for her if she
does decide she needs me."

"She just got hit with the one thing we fear the
most, so just give her time and space and as you
already said – keep her lifted in prayer. I'm sure she
didn't mean to be short with you when you spoke to
her, but she is dealing with a lot. She is truly in a
fight for her life. My advice to you would be to stay
in touch with her friends in Dallas caring for her, but
give her time to deal with all that she has ahead of
her. She knows that you care and that you are her
friend, which is why she reached out to you to let you
know her situation."

"You are right, as always," Joya said with sincere
appreciation.

Leaving the most complicated matter for last,
Naya turned Joya's chair to the face the mirror. When
Naya caught Joya's gaze in the reflection, she posed
the tough question, "What are you going to do about
David?"

Chapter 29

Joya vowed that this would be the last time she told the story about her vacation with David. Calling Sam was the last thing on her To-Do list before returning to work on Monday morning. Sam invited herself over to Joya's on Sunday afternoon. They were sitting in the morning room enjoying bubbly, sweet Prosecco and a smoked salmon platter that Joya prepared for them. Joya recounted the story for Sam that she had already told to Alise and Naya, beginning with the day tour of the island and ending with the sinister return of their belongings as they boarded their flight. She continued right on through, without stopping, to inform Sam of Alise's illness and Mona's relocation that she was hit with immediately upon her return.

Finally wrapping up the chronicles of the past few days for Sam, Joya sat back in her chair, waiting for her response. She had been looking forward to sharing the story with Sam, who was her best friend – she told her everything. Almost. She didn't tell her that she was falling in love with David.

"Girl! He bought you BLUE DIAMONDS?!" Sam asked with widened eyes and that piercing tone in her voice that unnerved Joya.

Seriously, Sam? 'Blue Diamonds' is all that you heard? And lower your voice! Joya raised from her relaxed pose, leaned towards Sam, and snapped her fingers as close to her eyes as she could as she shouted, "We were ROBBED! AT GUN POINT! Did you not hear anything after 'blue diamonds?' " She snapped her fingers once more for effect, then collapsed firmly against the back of her chair.

Laughing at Joya's reaction, Sam apologized, but her laughter only irritated Joya more. "Sam – this is NOT funny! WHY are you laughing?"

Composing herself, she apologized again. "I'm sorry. You're right – it's not funny. I wish you could have seen your face just now. But, seriously – I'm glad that you two are safe, and it wasn't worse because it could have been." They both sipped their wine, thinking of the next thing to say to each other. Joya was still talking herself out of being mad at Sam for laughing at her and decided she needed more wine to mellow out. While she poured more wine into her glass, she noticed Sam had recovered from her amusement and had fixed a noticeably serious gaze upon her.

"What?" Joya asked, surprised by the drastic mood change.

Sam was having a déjà vu moment, and she was hoping that she was wrong – but she didn't think so. She was rarely wrong when it came to reading Joya. She knew that it was touchy ground to tread, but not one to be fearful, she forged ahead with her concern.

"You are falling in love with him, aren't you?"

Part 2

Chapter 30

Joya turned to admire the purple dress reflected in the three-way mirror in the dressing room of the boutique that Mona discovered in Paris. She and William had been living there for two years, and they both loved it. This was Joya's third visit since Mona and William had relocated there. She came to help Mona plan their wedding and also visited for Mona's birthday last year.

"Not bad for almost forty," Joya said to her shapely image in the mirror. *How did forty come so fast? It seems like yesterday that I was graduating from High School.* A lot had happened in Joya's life since then...

She stepped out of the dressing room to show off the dress for Mona. "Beautiful!" Mona exclaimed. "It's gorgeous! You have to get it."

Joya laughed. "I like it, too! I think I'll wear it for my birthday party!"

Agreeing, Mona said, "Yes! It will be perfect! I have to find something to wear myself," she smiled, remembering that she promised Joya that she would come to the states to help her celebrate her milestone birthday in just a few short months from now. She had not been back to the U.S. since she and William arrived in Paris. She quickly fell in love with the city and loved being married to William. As much as she missed Joya, she hoped that they would be staying in Paris the full five years.

Deciding that it was time for lunch, Mona and Joya walked from the boutique to a Parisian café that Mona liked for the fresh salads and bread. She knew that Joya would also enjoy the wine. It was a perfect Fall day in Paris and Mona was feeling blessed to share it with her baby sister.

"So, how are the plans coming for your big celebration? I wish I was there to help you." Mona loved event planning and envisioned doing it full-time once she retired from her current profession as a Nurse Administrator.

"Everything is coming together. I just can't believe that I'm going to be FORTY!"

"You still look like you are in your twenties," Mona complimented her sister.

"Yeah – right! I don't FEEL like I'm in my twenties," Joya laughed. "I'm so blessed to still be so successful with my business, but I thought that I'd be married by now," Joya reflected.

"Marriage is not everything," Mona said sipping her water. She read Joya's questioning look. "No, I didn't mean it like that. I LOVE being married to William and our life here. I'm just saying that you shouldn't focus so much on NOT being married. It will come at the right time. Just be patient."

"That's easy for you say. You have the life you always dreamed of."

"I do, but I waited for it.   Also, I wasn't looking for William. HE found ME."

"I hear you, sister," Joya responded.

You hear me, but are you really listening? Mona didn't say what she was thinking.

Chapter 31

During the long flight from Paris back to Washington, D.C. Joya reflected the past few years of her life, the words of her sister echoing in her thoughts. *"I wasn't looking for William. HE found ME." I understand what she is saying, but I wasn't looking for Keith when he walked into the club that evening. I truly wasn't on the prowl for Bob Jones and his crazy life. Troy walked back into my life totally by surprise. And then there is David. Why does David have to be married? I'm glad that we decided to be friends, but when I think of us and the good part of our trip together...* Joya's heart melted when she remembered David's touch, their dance, and how much he wanted to love her despite his current circumstance.

As much as Joya wanted to be with David, she couldn't accept being with a married man or being in a clandestine relationship. She was a business woman very involved in the community, and she was not going to risk her reputation or devalue her self-worth. Not even for love. She hadn't been in a relationship since David. She was grateful that she had not submitted to having sex with him, although they had shared a special intimacy.

David was not pleased with Joya's decision not to see him anymore, but he couldn't argue with her. He was grateful that they at least would remain friends. He would miss her too much if not able to talk to her.

  Joya reclined her seat and closed her eyes as she continued to contemplate the meaning of her life. She had mixed feelings about turning forty. She was in good health, had good friends and a thriving business. There was still that one void in her life.

  She continued having a talk with herself. *I don't know how I created a pattern of attracting men with issues or that are not totally available to me. Bob: with his harem and children – a borderline polygamist; Keith: my soul-mate, but promised himself to another; David: my knight in shining armor – can't make a decision for his own life; Troy: a liar and a thief – Ugh! I have to do something different because whatever I've been doing is not working for me. I travel in circles with professional men, but most of them are married. The others are openly gay. What's a girl to do? Mona said that she wasn't looking for a relationship when William found her. I wasn't looking either when those crazy men appeared on my stage of life. Maybe it's my karma. Minister Srene said that 'we attract to us who we are.' Hmmm. All of them - Troy, Keith, Bob, and David are living their lives from a position of dishonesty. Troy never loved me at all, but is he any worse than the others? I need to examine what part of me is attracting unavailability. And dishonesty.*

  Joya suddenly felt a wave of nausea. It wasn't from the turbulence of the flight but from the turmoil of the internal discourse that led to the possible truth about herself.

Breathing deeply to hold the nausea at bay, she made a vow to herself that she would resolve her own faults before diving into another toxic relationship. She didn't think she could survive another one. She pledged to start the next decade of her life with a clean relationship slate, even if that meant being alone for a little while longer.

Chapter 32

Joya immersed herself in planning her fortieth birthday celebration. It was a pleasant distraction. When she wasn't working, she was planning her birthday event. Sam wondered why Joya was doing everything by herself when she had offered her help several times.

Joya wanted everything to be perfect. She had dedicated a special journal to capture her ideas and details. She carried it with her everywhere jotting down new inspirations as they emerged and checked off each task as it was completed.

It was time to send out the invitations that she created for her closest friends. The invitation would set the tone for the elegant soirée that she was planning. She selected seven heart-shaped Swarovski crystal necklaces, each heart in the color representing the birthstone of the individual girlfriends: Mona would receive Aquamarine; July Ruby for Alise and Pamela; most befitting to her personality, Sam would receive a rare Tourmaline; a rich green Emerald for Minister Srene and Naya would share the royal color purple Amethyst with Joya.

The indigo blue velvet box etched in the silver Swarovski logo was perfect for the invitation Joya designed. Each invitation was inscribed in blue ink on silver foil paper with a personal message to each of her friends. She carefully affixed the foil message to the inside lid of the elegant jewelry boxes. Mona's and Alise's invitations would have to be mailed but, she arranged for a courier to hand deliver the invitations, which were carefully packaged, to Sam, Pamela, Minister Srene and Naya. She laughed at the image in her mind of Sam receiving her package. Sam loved extravagance, and she would be blown away by Joya's personally designed invitation, which could only be weakly imitated, but definitely not duplicated.

She could hardly wait to receive Sam's reaction. She knew that Mona would be awestruck as would Naya. It was hard to guess with Pamela and Minister Srene, but she was sure they would accept the invitation to attend the special birthday celebration. Pamela had been her personal assistant and office manager shortly after she started her business. She was more than a personal assistant, always protective of her boss, not just because she was the source of her livelihood and the reason that she and her children could eat after her husband left, and she lost her job. Pamela genuinely admired Joya, cared for her and thought of her as a friend. Joya knew Pamela felt this way about her and was the reason she included her in the elite group to celebrate her birthday. It was rare to find such loyalty and Joya appreciated it in Pamela.

Joya didn't see Minister Srene often, but they shared a special bond of sisterhood and friendship that remained unchanged despite the passage of time between their encounters. Joya had often turned to her sister-friend, a Priest in an African based religion that she didn't understand, but there was no misunderstanding of the love and peace that emanated from Srene. Joya couldn't identify exactly what it was, but she was witness to how the ambiance of the room would transform to tranquility once Srene entered. Her tall, lean frame seemed to float when she walked. She respected everyone's individual religious beliefs and never attempted to persuade anyone to follow her ideals and convictions.

Pamela fondly thought of her friends as she relaxed with a contented smile. All of the invitations had gone out, and she eagerly anticipated her celebration in just four short weeks.

Chapter 33

He recognized the beautiful the woman sitting at the bar of the Waterfront Haven Restaurant. She usually came in with David Peterson. He knew David through their mutual friend, Teddy. Teddy introduced them when they were both at Blacks Sports Bar a couple of years ago for a special fight night event. He recognized David immediately as the gentleman that often had drinks with the lovely lady at the Waterfront Haven. After he was formerly introduced to David, he saw him and Joya a couple of times at the Haven and spoke briefly to the couple, mostly exchanging quick male chit chat with David while Joya usually had her head in the menu. He suspected that Joya wouldn't remember meeting him.

He also knew that Terri, the Restaurant Manager, always greeted Joya when she arrived at the restaurant and took special care to ensure she had the table of her choice as a business owner in the Harbor Complex and frequent customer. She apparently did not have a reservation today because she headed straight to the bar. She pulled out a small notebook and started flipping the pages, smiling as she wrote something.

He saw one of the bartenders, Josh move in her direction, and he politely intercepted him. Josh understood and quickly retreated in the opposite direction to check in with the customers on the other side of the circular bar. Joya looked up at the bartender standing in front of her. She was lost in her birthday planning journal and wasn't sure how long he had been standing there. He looked familiar; he must have served her before. She thought she knew all of the servers since she had been a regular customer for so many years.

"How are you? What can I get for you?" he asked smiling at Joya.

"I'm good. I'd like a Kir Royale - no twist, please," she requested.

"Absolutely," he quickly responded and headed to the other side of the bar to prepare Joya's drink, also noticing that she instantly went back to whatever she was doing in her little book. He returned, setting her drink atop a coaster. "One Kir Royale – no twist for the lady. Let me know if this is ok," he invited her to taste.

"Joya set her pen and journal on the bar, picked up the drink and took a sip. "This is perr-fect," she honestly responded. Pleased that she was pleased, he offered his hand, "I'm Bryce Sims."

Bryce Sims – where have I heard that name? Pushing aside her thoughts and accepting his hand, "I'm Joya," she said. "So, would you have not introduced yourself if I didn't like the drink?" she asked jokingly. *Nice looking guy,* she thought, noticing his nice smile, short beard against his pecan tan complexion and dark brown curly hair with the perfect hint of gray to match the gray tones already starting in his beard.

Bryce laughed with her. "Uhhh – I'm not sure." *She has a sense of humor.* Careful not to step outside of his bounds, "Enjoy your drink and let me know if you need anything else," he offered.

"Thanks," Joya said picking up her book and pen. Bryce observed her quietly talking on her cell phone and writing in her book. He was watching her glass so that he could be "Johnny-on-the-spot" when it was time to offer her another. As soon as there was one sip left in the glass, he approached her. "Can I get you another?"

"No, thank you," she said. "I'm driving, so one is my limit. I hope you don't mind if I sit here for a while? As long as it's not busy?"

Sit here for as long as you like, pretty lady. "Not at all. Sit for as long as you like. Would you like some sparkling water?" He thought he remembered seeing her and David drinking it before.

"Actually, I would like some sparkling water. Have you been my server before?" Joya didn't like to refer to people as 'servers', but she preferred that word to 'waiter.'

Bryce wanted to be honest with Joya. "No, I've never served you, but I met you once when you and your friend, David came in." He noticed the change in her expression. *Ouch!*

"Oh – I think I might remember." Jumping to conclusions, "So, you and David are friends?" she asked.

"No, I wouldn't say that we are friends. I know him through a mutual friend, Teddy Black, who owns Black's Sports Bar downtown D.C. I saw the two of you come in together a few times a while back." He reached under the counter for the sparkling water.

That was a while ago, Joya was feeling nostalgic. Bryce felt that he should change the subject slightly. "I also see you here with another lady – very professional and well dressed."

Joya knew he meant Samantha and perked up at Bryce's description. "That's my best friend, Samantha. We like it here, so this is one of our first choices when we want to hang out for good food and drinks. We like the atmosphere. I bring my clients here as well."

Good to hear. "Nice journal," he said noticing the unusual purple leather. Joya grabbed it and put it in her purse so that she wouldn't forget it. "Thanks. I like it, too. I picked it up in Paris last year and decided to use it to plan my fortieth birthday party." *Did I just tell this man that I'm turning forty?!*

Most women don't disclose their age. She must be as confident on the inside as she looks on the outside. Refreshing.

"Oh? What are you planning?" He was interested in hearing more about her birthday plans.

Joya filled him in on some of the details, careful not to share too much with a stranger. She liked talking to him; he seemed sincerely interested. That was a trait of a good bartender, she secretly mused. Feeling the need to shift the attention away from her, Joya looked to the rear of the restaurant where a beautiful spiral wrought iron staircase led to another level. She said to Bryce, "I've been here a thousand times, and I've always wondered where that staircase leads to."

"That leads to the boss' office and private dining area."

"Oh! Wow! Based on how the restaurant is decorated, I can only imagine that it is really nice up there."

It is. Bryce smiled at her and removed her empty water glass. "I'm going to close out for the evening. Your drinks are on me."

Chapter 34

True to expectation, Sam called Joya as soon as she arrived home from the Waterfront Haven. She knew the invitations would all be delivered by the end of the day.

"Joya! I cannot believe this beautiful invitation! And with my favorite Swarovski crystal jewelry! I cannot believe it! How did you ever think of this?"

You weren't the only one to get the jewelry, diva! Joya thought as she smiled in appreciation to Sam's obvious excitement. She was glad she'd invoked the reaction that she intended.

"I wanted to create something special and unique, so I just came up with that idea."

"I cannot wait for the party! No wonder you wouldn't let me help you. I can tell by the invitation that it will be my kind of affair. Who else is coming?" Sam demanded to know.

Joya laughed, "None of your business. Just have your glamorous, bedazzled ass where you need to be at the appointed time. And don't be late!" She removed the phone from her ear when Sam shrieked with laughter. *This is going to be a great event; money well spent.*

Alise received the jewelry box invitation two days later by express mail. Intrigued as to what Joya might be mailing to her, she excitedly opened the cardboard mailing box. The jewelry box had been surrounded in bubble wrap. *Only Joya*, Alise smiled. She finally got through the plastic bubbles to the blue velvet box, which she carefully opened. She gasped with delight when she saw the ruby colored crystal heart on the gold chain. *How beautiful!* She noticed the silver foil inside the box top.

Alise – Your friendship is a precious gift. I would be honored if you would join me as I celebrate my fortieth birthday and more than twenty years of friendship with you.

The sentiment brought Alise to tears. She loved Joya and cherished their friendship so much. Joya had come to Dallas a few months after her surgery to bring some normalcy back to her life. Alise appreciated all of her girlfriends coming to her rescue when she needed them the most: spending nights with her, making meals for her, and driving her to the hospital and appointments. Joya had no idea know how much her visit had meant to Alise. Joya always made her laugh, and she needed that after six months of chemo and losing her hair.

They enjoyed hanging out, getting massages, mani-pedis, walking through the mall, going out to dinner or just relaxing in front of the television sipping Sparkling Sangria that Joya mixed especially for them.

Saying a prayer of thanksgiving for a clean bill of health for the past two years, Alise was grateful that she would not miss Joya's big celebration. She would be on oral meds for the next three or four years, but it was manageable and a small price to pay for her good health. She wiped her tears, set the luxurious jewelry box on the counter and turned to her computer to make her flight reservations. Joya had indicated in the invitation that she had everything else covered. *Classic Joya style.*

Chapter 35

"Boss lady, it's almost time for you to meet Mr. Dukes at the Haven. Terri is on duty today and will have your table ready for you," Pamela informed her boss. She had made the reservation two weeks ago for Joya to meet with the potential client. She and Terri, the restaurant manager, had developed a special relationship since they spoke on the phone often for Joya's reservations. Normally, Pamela would not be able to afford a restaurant of that caliber, but Terri gave Pamela a significant discount when she came in. She just needed to know ahead of time because she would need to be there. It was a gesture of good will in appreciation for Joya's business. Terri also made sure that Joya always had the window table with a view of the Potomac and sometimes comped her drinks as well. She took pride in providing exemplary customer service for all customers, aware of the volatility of the restaurant business. There were a lot of restaurant choices at the National Harbor; she was grateful that Ms. Alexander chose to dine with them often.

Joya looked up from her birthday journal to the time displayed on her laptop. The big event was only two weeks away, and the excitement was building – for everyone. Pamela cried when she received the elegant invitation delivered to her home and was honored that her boss, that she loved so much, had included her in the festivities. She hoped that she would not disappoint her. "Oh! I better get moving! Thanks, Pamela. You always keep me on schedule," she said smiling at her assistant.

She grabbed her purse, briefcase and coat and headed for the elevator. It was February and extra cold outside when the wind blew over the Potomac River.

He held the elevator door open for her as she entered. Joya was not surprised to see David since his office was a few floors above hers. "Hey," she said. "How's it going?"

His heart still skipped a beat every time he saw Joya. "I'm good. Heading to lunch?" he asked.

"Yep - meeting with a potential client."

"Your birthday is coming up. Are you doing anything special?"

She smiled, thinking of her celebration. "As a matter of fact, I am." She told him about getting together with her girlfriends.

The elevator reached the street level; David held the door open for Joya to step out. "Maybe we can get together for drinks to celebrate?" he asked hoping that she would say 'yes.'

David's offer did not surprise Joya. "Thanks. We'll see. I'll let you know," she politely answered before turning to walk towards the Waterfront Haven. She pulled her collar around her neck to defend the wind. "See you later," she said ending the conversation.

Terri saw her approach and opened the side door to let Joya in so that she would not have to use the revolving door. "Hi, Ms. Alexander. Your table is ready. Can I take your coat for you?"

"Brrrr!" Joya said regarding the wind and chill outside. "Thanks, Terri," she said handing her coat and following her to her table. Joya had been a frequent customer for many years and was usually greeted by Terri. It clicked with her just then that her last name was 'Sims'; that must be why Bryce's name had been familiar to her when she met him a few weeks ago. When she was seated, she said to Terri, "I met your husband a couple of weeks ago when I was here. Nice guy; good bartender," Joya complimented.

Confused, Terri responded, "My husband is not a bartender."

Slightly embarrassed for jumping to conclusions, "Oh – I apologize. I thought that since he was working behind the bar…" Now understanding, Terri laughed, handing Joya a menu. "Oh, you mean Bryce. He's not – " She was interrupted by Mr. Dukes approaching the table.

Chapter 36

Joya liked Mr. Dukes, and it had been a good meeting, going a little longer than she planned. He was a family man, proud of his wife and children and talked about them freely. Joya admired that. She wanted that. But, she was not looking. She remembered what Mona said. Mr. Dukes agreed to the proposal for professional services presented by Joya and she was energized. She loved it when everything clicked with her and her clients. She prided herself on providing stellar customer service, and she looked forward to working with Mr. Dukes and his company.

It was late afternoon, so she decided to hang out at the Haven to have a drink to celebrate with herself. She had her laptop, so she set up shop at her table as she often did at the restaurant. It was so relaxing there, and the staff treated her well. Joya was respectful not to impose like that if it was busy, but on this Wednesday afternoon, the lunch crowd had dissipated, and it would be a couple of hours before the dinner crowd started coming in.

The staff had become familiar with Joya. Her server noticed that Mr. Dukes had left, and Joya had her laptop out and had begun to work. She had settled the lunch check, but he would ask if she need anything. Joya ordered her usual Kir Royale – no twist and settled in to celebrate her success and to catch up on her emails.

Bryce noticed Joya sitting by the window as he walked down the stairs. He had arrived at the restaurant earlier during the busy lunch rush and went straight to his office. He was glad to see her, but she looked busy, so he would not approach her – just yet.

Joya lost herself in her work and had blocked the rising sound of customers coming in for dinner. She looked at the time on her laptop. *Oh, my! It's five-thirty! I didn't mean to sit her so long! I need to get out of here.* As she packed her laptop in her briefcase, she noticed Sam sitting at a table across the other side of the restaurant. She was animatedly engaged in conversation with a handsome Caucasian gentleman who Joya guessed to be a co-worker. She didn't recognize him, but there had been lots of personnel changes since she'd left the law firm many years ago. She would go over to say 'hello.'

Bryce thought that Joya was heading towards the door, but she curved instead towards the other side of the restaurant. He immediately understood why when he saw the lady who was Joya's friend.

Sam did not see Joya approach, but recognized the voice calling out, "Hi - Samantha!" Joya referred to Sam by her proper name since she was obviously with a co-worker. Turning to the gentleman, Joya introduced herself. "Hi, I'm Joya Alexander," she extended her hand. He stood and gently shook Joya's hand.

"I didn't mean to interrupt your meeting," Joya said to the gentleman, "but I saw my best friend and just wanted to say, 'hi.' " He projected a questioning look to Sam as he re-seated himself. "It's nice to meet you, Joya. I'm Richard Singleton. My friends call me 'Rich.' I've heard a lot about you," he reported. Joya took her turn with the confused look directed to Sam. *Huh? Why have you heard a lot about ME?* Before she could finish her thought and open her mouth to insert her other foot, Joya noticed the wine glasses on the table. She knew that Sam NEVER drinks with co-workers or clients of her law firm.

Ouch! Joya heard loudly and clearly in her head. She wanted so badly to retreat with her dignity to still intact, but Sam was not having it. Joya was her best friend, but her privacy had been invaded which Joya clearly read in her eyes and detected in her voice when she said, "Joya – Rich is my DATE. Thanks for stopping by. I'll call you later?"

Joya knew there was no way to recover, so she quickly said, "Oh sure! I'm so sorry...I didn't mean to interrupt...Rich – so nice to meet you." She returned the steely glare to Sam, "YES – Sam. We WILL talk later." She was angry not only by the embarrassment, but also because Sam had not told her that she was dating anyone! As she headed towards the door, her flushed color increased with her thoughts. *I cannot believe that she is dating someone, and she didn't tell me! I tell her EVERYTHING! I can't believe that her date is a WHITE guy! Sam!*

He IS handsome...

Chapter 37

Bryce observed how quickly Joya was heading to the door. He headed in her direction, calling out, "Joya!" She turned just as she reached the door to see the bartender she met before, Bryce. *Not now! I have got to get out of here!* She didn't want to be impolite, so she stopped in her tracks to speak to Bryce. "Hi. How are you?"

He noticed her flushed cheeks and wondered what happened at the table with her friend. "I'm good. Are you okay?" he asked, concerned.

"Um – I'm not sure," she answered honestly. Thinking quickly, he suggested, "Hey – I was about to take a break. Would you like to sit with me for a few minutes?"

Escaping was the forefront of Joya's mind. "Thanks, but I need to go." She looked outside, and a light rain had started to fall. She didn't have an umbrella, and she was not in the mood to get wet considering the cold wind also blowing. "You wouldn't have an umbrella, would you?"

"I do. Wait here while I get it for you."

"Wait – " Joya said. "I'll have a drink with you if the invitation is still open." She thought she could use the time to compose herself. Bryce could not have been happier, and he led her to an open table near the rear of the restaurant. Joya didn't like it back there because it was dark and not near the windows with a view of the Potomac, but right now, dark without a view would work perfectly for her.

Bryce pulled her chair out, assisting her to get comfortably seated at the small table for two before taking his seat on the other side. "Are you sure you are okay?" he asked her again.

She decided to be honest with him. "I'm just a little embarrassed," she confessed. She gave him the quick version of what happened with Sam and Rich starting with her assumption that it was a business meeting and ending with, "I can't believe that didn't tell me she was dating someone!" Glad to hear that it was nothing serious, he said, "Wow! Wait here – I'll be right back." He returned with a beer for himself and a Kir Royale for Joya. He remembered she liked it without the lemon twist. She laughed when he returned, but appreciated the gesture. It had been a while since she had enjoyed the drink she ordered earlier, so she accepted it. She lifted it in a toast to Bryce's beer.

He took a sip of his beer and watched as Joya sipped the drink he made especially for her. When she placed her glass on the table, he leaned forward and asked, "So – are you most upset that your BFF is dating, and you didn't know...or is it the part about him being white?"

Bryce's jagged questions, delivered with natural wit, transformed Joya's annoyance and embarrassment to amusement, which she very much appreciated. But, her internal alarms sounded in her head immediately thereafter. This danger zone she was entering was all too familiar, and she vowed never to enter it again. She had no interest in Bryce and had no idea why he was being so nice to her other than he knew that she was a frequent customer. She started to gather her belongings, "Bryce – thanks," she said. "I needed the laugh; and the drink. But, I have to go."

Bryce didn't know what triggered the abrupt change and certainly didn't see it coming. "Why? What's wrong?" he asked touching her arm, making Joya more uncomfortable.

"Look, I appreciate you giving me special treatment because I'm a regular customer, but I don't want your wife to get the wrong idea," she said directly, making sure that he understood her position.

Not understanding, "My wife?" Bryce questioned. *WHAT is she talking about?* "I'm not married," he added. Joya stepped back to look at him directly. He towered at least a foot over her five-foot, petite frame. "Seriously?" she accused. "Terri is not your wife?"

Bryce burst into laughter and had to catch his breath, but knew he had to recover quickly as Joya turned redder with each passing moment. "Terri is my sister!"

Chapter 38

Joya drove into work the next morning with her feelings of embarrassment still surrounding her. She was mad at herself for jumping to conclusions with both Sam and Bryce. Her cell phone was ringing in her purse, and she was not able to reach it while driving, which added to her irritation. She despised starting her day in a funk like this.

WHO is calling me this early in the morning?! Joya retrieved her phone from her purse when she came to a stop at the red light one block from her office parking garage. The missed call was from Sam. "Oh – so NOW you want to talk to me?" Joya said aloud, slamming the phone back into her purse. The car behind her tooted the horn for her to go; the light had changed to green. "Don't rush me!" she yelled at the driver's image in her rearview mirror.

Pamela immediately sensed her boss' mood when she entered the office. She would cautiously wait a little bit before delivering her cup of green tea. *I don't know what has her panties in a bunch, but I'm staying away until the coast is clear!*

After mumbling 'Good morning' to Pam, Joya immediately went into her office and shut the door. She dialed Sam from her office phone. "It's about time you called me back," she answered on the first ring. "Did you listen to my voice mail?"

"Good morning to you, too. No, I didn't listen to your voice mail. What's up?" Joya asked, not in the mood for Sam's telephone games.

Oh, boy. She is in a mood today. "I was calling to see if you want to have lunch today?"

Seriously – you want to have lunch? "Thanks, but no."

"I'm treating! Come on, Joya!" Sam pleaded.

"Sam, I'm not in the mood." Getting to the point, "So, why didn't you tell me that you are dating someone?" Joya questioned. "If you had run up on me with someone that you didn't know, you would have thrown a hissy fit! Do you know how embarrassed I was when he told me that he had heard a lot about me, but I obviously knew NOTHING about him?"

Sam could hear Joya's hurt feelings. She knew that she should have told her about Rich, but she feared being judged. As close as they were, she didn't want to disclose that she preferred dating men outside of her race. It wasn't a prejudice - she just found them more interesting. She didn't want this incident to cause a rift in her relationship – with Joya or with Rich.

Deciding to be honest with her best friend, "I didn't want you to judge me because I like dating white men," Sam said. "I like men of all races, as a matter of fact. It's just that African-American men don't appeal to me. I have a right to like what I like."

Joya's blood was boiling. "All this time I've known you, and you NEVER shared that with me! You know almost everything about me and all of the wretched details of my failed relationships. AND – what makes you think that I would judge you? We are SUPPOSED to be friends! I don't care WHAT or WHO you like. But it doesn't make you better because you prefer to date other races!"

They were both treading on shaky ground with each other. Joya decided to bring it back. "Look, Sam. I don't mean to come off this way, but I have to be honest and tell you that my feelings were hurt to find out that you are dating someone that you obviously like, but you didn't tell me. I'm supposed to be your BFF. We obviously have different preferences when it comes to men, but I don't begrudge your right to choose and your happiness. Plus, if you are not going for the brothas, that means more choices for me," Joya added with humor. As hurt as she was, she did not want this incident to negatively impact their friendship. Sam was not totally out of the dog house with Joya, but she was willing to give her some slack. *Men come and go, but girlfriends are forever.*

Sam laughed, glad to know that they were getting back on track. She knew how hard it was for Joya to trust and hoped that the trust between them remained intact.

"We've only been dating for a few weeks, but I have a lot to catch you up on!" Sam reported with a smile.

Chapter 39

"So, what's going on with you, man? You've been nursing that same beer for an hour. That's not like you – you would normally be on at least number four or five by now," Teddy said to David, partially joking although he detected something in his mood. They had been sitting at the bar watching football for a couple of hours.

"I don't know, man. Life is crazy, I guess."

"You still got issues at home?"

"Nope. Lynn and I are done. We finally split. I moved out."

Teddy was not prepared to hear this news from his friend. He had been lamenting about his home life for years and never took any steps towards improving his life. Not even when he had a chance with Joya.

"Really? When?" he inquired, interested in hearing the details.

"A couple of weeks ago. Lynn is just nasty. She has everything that any woman could want. Nice house; luxury cars; two beautiful kids; she didn't have to work – but now she does. I could no longer live with someone who only wanted to talk to me about the kids. She was never affectionate towards me and forget cooking any meals for me; she only cooked enough for her and the kids."

Teddy recognized David for the good guy that he was and felt sorry for his unfortunate situation. "I just don't get that, man." He knew that David had lost his chance with Joya a couple of years ago after their trip together, but maybe now... "So, what's up with Joya? Did you tell her?"

"Naw...I didn't tell her. I want to, but she is planning her birthday celebration, and I don't want to get in the way and spring this on her. I don't know how she will feel after so much time has passed. We're still friends, and I definitely want to see if we can have a relationship; I still care about her, but I don't know...what do you think?" David asked, almost desperate for Teddy's opinion.

Teddy took a thoughtful swig from his beer, then turned and looked directly at David. "I think you should go for it."

Chapter 40

After months and months of planning, the big day finally arrived kicking off the weekend celebration. Joya awakened with a smile on her face and fell onto her knees in prayer. She had so much to be thankful for, and she wanted God to know before she did anything else. She thanked Him for her health and strength, for her family and friends, for her prosperity in business and for all that He brought her through to reach the pivotal age of forty. She requested continued guidance and direction, mercy, grace, and favor. Through her tears, she asked that God continue to bless her sweet Delia and Louis with unconditional love, joy, peace and all the gifts of His glorious kingdom.

Alise was landing at Washington, D.C. International Airport. Mona arrived the day before and accompanied Joya to pick up Alise. With both women and their luggage in tow, Joya drove from the airport to the Gaylord National Hotel where the four-bedroom Presidential Suite had been reserved for her, Mona, Sam and Alise; a three-bedroom suite for Pamela, Minister Srene and Naya. She put a lot of energy and love in planning a celebration that none of them would forget.

Two valets appeared to open the car doors for the ladies, and a third was already at the rear, prepared to unload their luggage. Joya had already checked in for both rooms; the hotel staff was aware of who she was and the money she was spending for the weekend. Pamela took off of work early to help Joya with last minute details and was looking forward to a weekend of not being on "mommy duty," but was more than happy to continue her assistant duties for her boss. It was different, though, helping Joya with her party; it didn't feel like work, but more like helping a friend.

"Wow!" Alise exclaimed when she exited the front passenger side of Joya's BMW. "We are staying HERE?" she asked.

"Yes, ma'am!" Joya beamed. "We are celebrating in high style this weekend!" Mona smiled with appreciation as she joined the ladies to walk into the front door of the hotel, held open by the doorman.

They giggled like school girls all talking at once on the elevator ride to the nineteenth floor. Joya handed her key to the bellman and followed him down the long hallway to the Presidential Suite. Alise and Mona 'oohed' and 'ahhed' when they stepped into the grand foyer that was bigger than some small apartments they'd seen.

"Joya, this is beautiful!" Alise said. Mona concurred, "My sister REALLY KNOWS how to do it!" she complimented. She was so glad that she came to celebrate with her Joya. She already missed William, but it was only for a few days. She didn't realize how much she missed the States until now.

Joya was in her element as she led the ladies on a tour of the grand suite. As they'd previously planned, Pamela met the ladies when they arrived in the dining area with a glass of champagne. She had also taken care of having a light fare catered for them, as also instructed by Joya. The food would be delivered from hotel catering in an hour, just in time for the other ladies to arrive. Their room was one floor down, on eighteen, but Pamela had called and instructed them to come directly to Joya's suite. Joya had already checked them in, had their keys, and they could settle in later.

Pamela knew Mona, of course, but had not met Alise – she had only talked to her on the phone and didn't care for her very much. The feeling was mutual. Pamela thought that Alise could be demanding and rude. Alise thought that, although she had come a long way, Pamela was still a little ghetto. They both inwardly vowed to be on their best behaviors for Joya this weekend and not wear their feelings for each other on their sleeves.

The ladies were still in animated conversation when they heard the doorbell ring. Pamela jumped to get it so that Joya could enjoy her guests without interruption. Sam led the way in her signature flashiness, followed by Naya and Srene, who arrived on time and at the same time. Although she didn't need to be, Sam was dressed like the party was that evening in one of her classic St. John knit outfits. Tonight, she modeled a black and gold two-piece pants outfit; of course with matching shoes and purse. "O-M-G, Joya! This is so FAB-U-LOUS!" she exclaimed, commanding the attention and conversation.

Sam's voice always grated on Mona's nerves, but she was careful not to show what she was thinking in her mind on her face. *She is so loud! Shut up with that voice! Ugh!*

Pamela served champagne to the other ladies, so pleased to see the smile on Joya's face and especially grateful to be a part of her special celebration. Srene and Naya managed to get words in to echo everyone else's appreciation and admiration of the accommodations. They could only imagine what was yet to come.

Chapter 41

The food arrived right on time, but that didn't interrupt the gaiety and spirited chatter of the ladies. Joya was so glad that she decided to have the celebration. Srene offered the blessing of the food, and everyone jumped right to it; they worked up quite an appetite just from talking. And drinking.

Srene waited for the appropriate time when everyone was resting from feasting on the delicious buffet and had their glasses full, she proposed a toast to Joya.

Standing in her personal aura of light, and dressed in one her colorful African outfits, Srene addressed the group, "Everyone, I would like to toast our hostess and birthday celebrant," she said tapping her fork against her glass. She continued, "We are here to honor our sister, Joya. Joya, I'm grateful to you for your friendship and for all that you are in the world. Here's to another forty years of God's love and prosperity."

They all raised their glasses in salute to Joya. Naya sipped her champagne, also silently thanking God for their friendship. She admired Joya and was curious about what was yet to come for her. "I agree. Joya, you deserve all that life has to offer. What's next for you? Any romance on the horizon?" Naya asked.

Joya cringed at that the word 'romance.' She looked at Mona, then Sam. "Thank you Srene and Naya." To address Naya's specific question, "As for romance, I'm going to take my sister's advice." She answered.

Curious, Naya looked at Mona. "Really? What was your advice?"

Mona was proud to report the advice she gave to her sister a few months ago. "I told my sister that she deserves a man that will love her without condition and without COMPLICATION."

Ouch, Naya thought, knowing Joya's saga with men. Mona continued, "I suggested that she stopped looking and let HIM find HER."

"Good advice," Naya agreed.

Sam had to interject her two cents worth. "In the meantime, you should date just for fun. You can't just work all the time and not have any fun!" *She has a good point,* Joya thought, but not without noticing the dagger that Mona threw Sam with her looks.

In quick response to deflect the tension between the ladies, Joya remarked, "You are doing pretty good on the dating scene. Ladies, guess what - Sam is dating! A rich-looking white guy," she announced, not able to resist. All eyes simultaneously turned to Sam. Joya laughed, "How did you meet this wonderful guy anyway?" Sam had not shared those details with her.

"What?" she said to the ladies whose eyes were still fixed upon her. "I don't have a right to choose who I want to date?" Turning to Joya, "I met him online if you must know! You should try it. You just might meet someone you like!"

"Online?! I don't believe that you are using those dating sites! Are you crazy?" Joya screamed at her.

Pamela, Naya, Srene, and Alise enjoyed the exchange between Sam and Joya. Mona remained neutral, wanting to see where the conversation was going. Pamela was feeling more comfortable and one with the group when she broadcasted, "Yeah, Boss Lady. That's how I met Sergio – online!"

"Sergio?!" everyone roared in unison.

"Oh, yes! He used to be an exotic dancer!"

Only Pamela, Joya joined the others in laughter. "Don't you mean 'stripper?' Let's call it what it is!" Alise said through her laughter. Pamela rolled her eyes at Alise in response.

Alise recovered from her laughter openly sharing, "Joya, I met my current 'friend' online, too. You have to be careful, of course, but you have to be careful anyway. 'Crazy' could be anywhere. You SHOULD try it." Turning to Pamela, "Can you stop calling her 'Boss Lady?' " Alise demanded, a little tipsy. A little hurt at first, Pamela quickly recovered answering, "Ok. Just for this weekend, I will call her by her name, but come Monday, it's back to 'Boss Lady.' " Pamela was not going to let Alise win. Naya laughed, mostly with Pamela and not at her. She could empathize with her somewhat because Joya started as her customer, but they had become close friends.

Joya was surprised that almost everyone in the room had tried online dating sites except her. She was glad to hear that that Alise was dating again and rubbed her a bit. "Uh huh! I see you, 'Miss Thing' showing off your perky cleavage and a new hair weave!"

"Darn right, I'm showing them off. The real ones were never this perky!" Alise said puffing her cleavage more and flipping her new hair. The light brown color was a striking contrast to her dark brown skin. Joya was glad that Alise received her comment as the compliment that she intended.

"Naya, what do you think?" Joya asked. She laughed with the group, but wasn't saying much.

"You wouldn't believe how many clients I have that found their mates online. A few of them have even gotten married," Naya responded to Joya's direct question.

Srene added, "That's right. I was just going to say that I've counseled and performed the wedding ceremonies for several couples that met online. It seems to be the way that busy professionals like yourselves are meeting quality men."

"Mona, you've been quiet; what do you think?" Joya asked, interested in her sister's opinion.

"I'm just glad that I met William when I did. I don't think I would know how to be single today. Since you LIVE on the internet anyway, maybe you should try one of the more exclusive sites. But, remember: let the man come to YOU."

Time passed quickly as the group moved from one lively discussion to the other. When it was after midnight, Joya stood and announced, "Happy Birthday to ME! I'm going to bed so that I'm rested for the main celebration tomorrow." The ladies stood and encircled her in a group hug.

Pamela, buzzing from hours of sipping champagne was the first to emerge from the huddle. "This ain't the party?" she slurred. Everyone laughed; Joya shook her head humorously at Pamela and bid them all goodnight.

When she was sure that everyone was settled in their rooms, Joya relaxed in her room saying a silent prayer before drifting off to sleep, *Thank you, God for blessing me with the gift of sisterhood and friendship.*

Chapter 42

Joya arose earlier than planned, being too excited to sleep through the night. She went into the living room of the suite and quietly opened the drapes to the view of the sun shining brightly over the Potomac. *What a beautiful day; thank you, God.* She brewed a cup of green tea for herself, quietly so as not to wake Alise, Mona, and Sam. They had a late night, plus she wanted a few minutes to herself before embarking on the next segment of her celebration.

It wasn't long before the others rose; they were also excited to celebrate with Joya. As previously instructed, they all met in Joya's suite once they were dressed. All they knew was that they were to meet at ten-thirty a.m. for brunch; Joya had not disclosed the details beyond that. They all remembered to wear the heart necklace that they received in their invitations.

Joya, dressed in the regal purple dress she purchased in Paris, covered by a black cashmere and faux fur cape, led the delegation down to the hotel lobby and through the front door where a white limo waited to drive them two short blocks to the waterfront. They probably could have walked, but Joya did not want them to have to fight the bitter cold and wind of mid-February. Mona and Sam were beautiful and warm in their full length furs, and the other ladies also dressed for the bitter cold, but Joya decided that they would ride in high-style even for the short distance.

Sam loved traveling luxuriantly and was the first to relax into the plush leather of the stretch limo, followed by Joya, Mona, Alise, Naya, Srene and Pamela, who didn't miss her opportunity to flirt with the young, handsome driver. The chauffer smiled at the ladies, closed the door and set off for the very short drive. When they reached the pier, Pamela saw the Elite Charter Cruise private yacht docked and ready. It was a beautiful vessel: gleaming white, one hundred twenty-four feet long with large panoramic windows, four open-air decks, and four private dining rooms. Joya had rented one of the smaller private rooms for her celebration.

The driver opened the door to allow the squealing ladies to exit and smiled as he watched them scurry towards the ship. Joya led the way, giving her name as she was greeted by the hostess who led them to their private dining room. Joya was awestruck by the beauty of the room and that every detail she requested had been carried out to perfection. The long dining table was set with red linens, white china and gold flatware. The cut crystal glasses sparkled with the crystal chandelier overhead. Three brilliantly sparkling etched crystal vases held mixtures of red and lavender roses. Pleased, Joya took her seat at the head of the table and invited her guests to also be seated.

At the head of each place setting was a place card with the name of each of her girlfriends. Beside the place card, a pewter frame trimmed in pearls and rhinestones displayed a photo of Joya and the girlfriend to be seated there. Mona was the first to notice amid the constant chatter and excitement. The photo of her and Joya, taken at least thirty years ago was of them dressed in their pink and white dresses, with matching white gloves and white patent leather shoes, on their way to Easter service at their church. She choked with emotion and hugged her sister.

One-by-one, the ladies absorbed the sentiment of their individual photo with the birthday celebrant. The adoration that Joya intended for each of her girlfriends was not missed and the specially selected photos were just the beginning.

It was tough because everyone was talking, but Joya managed to get their attention. "Ladies, I just want to formally thank you all for being a special part of my life and for being here to celebrate me turning forty in all of my fabulousness! The celebration today will be modeled after Oprah and will feature 'my favorite things.' Of course we have to begin with champagne!" On cue, the server assigned to the party poured them each a glass and moved right onto serving them their first course, which they each chose from the menu listing Joya's favorite salads and soups; the main course entrée selections consisted of herbed salmon, roasted turkey breast, and lobster tails with baked potatoes and steamed mixed vegetables.

Right before dessert was to be served, Srene led the group in a prayer for Joya. Sam followed by presenting Joya with a gift that was beautifully wrapped in shimmering blue paper topped with a silver bow that followed the color scheme of the invitation. "We didn't know that the theme of today would be your favorite things, but we all got together and agreed that this would be the perfect gift for you."

Joya carefully opened the box to find gift cards to six of her favorite places to shop. She could not have been more pleased. "Oh my God! This is perfect! I can hardly wait to go shopping! Thank you all SO MUCH!" Mona contributed to the joint gift, but also had a special gift for her sister, which she pulled from her leather bag.

"Joya, I have a little something extra for you," she said presenting her with the blue velvet box, much like the one the invitation had come in.

Always such a show-off! Sam thought regretting that she had not gotten Joya a separate gift as well. Joya opened the box to display a beautiful bracelet of precious stones arranged in rows of random color. "It's perfect! I love it!" she said placing the bracelet on her arm.

"Although it's my birthday, I am taking this opportunity to celebrate all of you and what you mean to me. This is a celebration of US."

Chapter 43

They reached the Georgetown Waterfront and while the other passengers departed the ship to explore the historic city for ninety minutes, Joya and her guests remained in the private dining room, still celebrating. The staff kept the champagne flowing and stayed close by to deliver anything they needed.

Joya planned the celebration especially to honor her sister and her closest friends. She started with Mona, choking back the emotion when she said, "Mona, you are my one and only sister, and I could not have asked for a better one. I thank God every day and every night for blessing me with YOU. I've always looked up to you – wanted to be you. You have always supported me in everything I've ever done, no matter how hair-brained it might have been," Joya said laughing. "I wish that everyone could be blessed with a sister like you. You are truly the wind beneath my wings, and I love you for it. "

Mona reached over and kissed Joya with the love and appreciation genuinely unique to the two of them.

"Alise, you have been my friend since college and despite the physical distance between us, we remain close by our heartstrings. Although we don't talk every day, when we do talk, it's as if no time has passed at all. Thank you for being an example to all of us what it means to be a fighter. When your body threw you a curve ball, you put up a good fight, and you won. I so admire you for your courage. I celebrate you, and I love you."

Alise winked at Joya in response.

Moving on to Sam, "Some people would say that Sam and I became friends by accident, meeting at work, but Srene would tell you that it was no fluke," Joya said. "But - God has everything in Divine order according to His perfect and Divine will for us. You have been my road chick since we met, and you have laughed and cried me through so much craziness in my life. I'm so grateful to you for not judging me and not actually slapping me even when you threaten to. There have been times when you SHOULD have slapped me back to reality," Joya joked, and Sam laughed through her tears. "You know I love you in all of your diva-ness," Joya added.

It was a rare occasion for Sam to be rendered speechless; this was one of those times that she had no words. She conveyed a smile to Joya revealing what she felt in her heart – love for her friend.

Directing her attention the other side of the table to Srene, "So many times I felt like I just wanted to give up, and all I needed was a dose of Minister Srene," Joya smiled. "I have never met anyone as calm as you are, and I thank you for listening to me and counseling me through all my 'stuff.' Everyone needs someone that they can be totally transparent with, and you are that friend. Thank you, and I love you."

"I love you too," she blew a kiss to Joya. "You don't realize what a blessing you are."

"Naya, you have been my sounding board for many years, and I never imagined that this friendship would have developed from you being my hairstylist. Because I'm older, it would seem that I would be the one giving you advice, but it's usually the other way around. You have the gift of wisdom beyond your years on this earth, and it amazes me! When I think about it, we very rarely talk face-to-face, because you are usually standing behind me styling my hair while we talk. That is symbolic to me of you always having my back. Thank you. I love you."

Naya returned the sentiment, adding, "It is YOU that I admire. You may not realize it, but I've learned a lot just by observing you. And talking to you. I admire your strength and resilience, and I pray the Creator will continue to bless you as you continue to be a blessing."

Joya was getting emotional, but she had to keep going. Pamela was the last one and was already crying through her rough exterior. She was the classic example of someone's bark being worse than their bite. "Miss Pamela – what can I say about you?" Joya smiled at her. "You are my protector on a daily basis, and I know that you would do anything for me. When I lost my way with my company a while back, you held it all together the best way that you could, and I don't know if I ever thanked you for it. Right now, in this moment, I want you to know how much I so appreciate you. You have more talent than you give yourself credit for. I am honored to be your 'boss lady' and your friend."

Pamela shot a look at Alise when Joya publicly condoned the moniker she often used to refer to Joya. Alise returned the snarled look back to Pamela, which made everyone laugh. Pamela regained her composure to respond to what Joya had just said to her. "Boss Lady – Joya: you saved my life so many years ago when I had run out of options. When I called you and said that I needed a job, you instantly invited me to come and work for you without skipping a beat. That was many years ago, and I have not forgotten it. Yes, I will do ANYTHING for you. Anyone trying to get to you has to come through me. I've learned a lot from you, and I like to think that I've evolved over the years under your tutelage, but I will still get STREET if I have to!"

They were all overcome with emotion, but Joya continued through it. "Now, I have something for all of you," she said reaching under the table for the bag that had been placed there for her by the cruise staff. "Life is a journey, and we should be grateful for it. So, I'm giving you each a journal, to write down your dreams and aspirations and also what you are grateful for. I've already written the first passage in each one, saying how grateful I am for each of you. Before the end of the day, I'm asking that you write in each other's journal." She handed them each a blue leather journal inscribed in silver: *Good Friends -*

Good Times. On the first page of each one, she had already written a personal note that began with, *'My prayer for you...'*

This gesture brought Srene to tears. "Thank you, Joya," she said getting up from her chair, coming to Joya and embracing her in a loving hug. She kept her arm around her and turned to the ladies seated at the table. "We all know how special Joya is, but I admire her for her strength and tenacity, but mostly for her faith. A lot of people would have crumbled under the weight of what she has endured, but here she stands strong and beautiful," she said hugging her again while the others applauded. Srene was Joya's counsel through the death of her parents, the devastation of her company and everything else that had transpired in her life over the years. She truly respected how she had come through her obstacles and grown from them.

Joya took her seat and retrieved yet another blue velvet box from her bag; this one tiny in size. "This is my final gift. I hope that it conveys what I feel in my heart for you." The ladies opened their boxes and harmoniously expressed inexplicable emotion when they saw the heart-shaped gold charm inscribed: *'BFF Forever – Love Joya.'* Slightly larger than the crystal heart, Joya instructed them that both were to be worn together, the newest one a backdrop to the sparkling heart that they were wearing that was sent with the invitation.

Too overwhelmed with emotion to place the charms on their necklaces, the ladies once again enfolded Joya in a heartfelt embrace. Pamela gushed with tears but managed to say, "No one has ever done anything like this for me before – thank you, Joya."

After enjoying more of Joya's favorite things, including chocolate dipped strawberries and cheesecake with fresh berries for dessert, the ladies stumbled to the main deck for line dancing during the last hour of the cruise. Seeing her friends enjoy and celebrate made Joya smile as they all moved on the dance floor together. Even Alise and Pamela seemed to be getting along. And there was hope yet for Mona and Sam.

She artistically danced across the floor with the ladies she cherished so much remembering something that she read about girlfriends: *Friends are connected heart to heart; distance can't break them apart.*

Chapter 44

I'm glad that my celebration was last weekend and not THIS weekend, Joya thought as she watched the sky pouring heaps of snow. This was unusual for the Metropolitan area, and after the first ten inches had fallen, the area was crippled. Joya called Pamela earlier in the morning when she heard the forecast predicting a two-foot accumulation before stopping. She asked her to call the other support staff to let them know the office would be closed today and until further notice.

By noon, Joya was bored having already had lunch and catching up on her e-mails. She remembered the conversation she had with her girlfriends about online dating. *Should I? Shouldn't I?* she contemplated. *I shouldn't,* she decided, then dialed Sam.

"Hey, girl. What are you doing during this blizzard?" Joya asked when Sam answered. Sam whispered something in the phone that Joya couldn't understand. She heard her the second time when she said, "I'm snowed in with Rich."

"Oh!" Joya reacted, surprised. "Sorry! Call me when you are free. Enjoy yourself, girl," Joya added before hanging up. *She is snowed in with her man!*

Damn! Everybody has a man except me! She remembered Mona's advice. She wouldn't look for anyone...exactly... She flipped her laptop back open and searched for the dating sites that the other ladies recommended. She would stay away from the one where Pamela met Sergio; *no male exotic dancers for me.* She checked out the site that Alise used, deciding it was too open. It appeared too much like a shopping site. Moving on to the site that Sam used, she found it much more secure, and it seemed to cater to professionals. Members have to use their real names, and there is no 'shopping'; she would need to sign up and create an account just to browse the possibilities. She pulled the credit card from her purse that she used for online transactions and created a thirty-day account. *Here goes...*

Not bad, Joya thought as she perused profiles of several handsome, professional men. *I can see why Sam used this site.* Having satisfied her curiousity, she heard a ping as she was about to sign off. It was a wink from 'Zack.' Surprised, Joya clicked on his name to access his full profile. She found they are the same age, he is also a business owner – two things in common so far; a divorcee, with one son, he enjoys sports. His photo was a headshot of an average looking, medium brown complexion professional man, dressed in a dark suit and tie.

Hmmm...maybe I'll wink back. Joya returned the online flirt that resulted in an hour of online communication with Zack. It felt safe, and it was fun. Zack asked when they could meet, which put Joya on guard. *Great talking to you - let's talk again soon,* she typed then signed off. She called Alise to get some advice from a veteran online dater.

Alise answered on the first ring, without saying hello, "I see on the news all the snow dumping on you guys," she reported. "Yes!" Joya responded. "I was so bored, so guess what I've been doing for the past hour?"

Delighted to hear that Joya was open to her recommendation of trying online dating, she agreed that she had done the right thing cutting off communication with Zack at the suggestion of meeting, but advised that it was not necessarily a red flag. "I think you should chat with him again, but wait a couple of days, and let him know that you want to take it slow. If he agrees, then make plans to meet him. In a public place, of course," Alise advised.

"Sounds like a plan. I'll keep you posted on how it goes," Joya accepted the directive, and then brought Alise up-to-speed on where Sam was spending her snow day in the nation's capital.

Chapter 45

Pamela walked to Joya's office, buttoning her coat, ready to call it a day. *Thursday evening and only one more day before my weekend starts,* she thought. She poked her head into Joya's office, informing her, "I'm getting ready to leave unless you need anything else."

"No, I'm good. I'm getting ready to leave myself." She was meeting Zack in person for the first time after chatting with him online for the past month. The weather continued to be brutal, and it was mid-March before any reprieve. David called her about once a week, asking if they could get together, but the weather never cooperated. Joya was glad, but over him and excited to meet Zack, planning for a fresh start on the dating scene. The weather also gave Joya a good excuse to delay the in-person meeting with Zack.

The time had come to meet him and she was excited, but nervous at the same time. She decided to share her news with Pam. "Guess what? I'm meeting a guy this evening for drinks that I met online," she announced.

Pam was surprised to hear the news from her boss, but honored that she shared with her. She could tell that she was nervous about it and offered her some advice. "Okay, so here is what I want you to do," Pamela began her instruction. She had more experience in this area than her boss and felt confident advising her in this area. "Only have one drink with him and then let him know that you have another commitment. That will give you an escape if you don't like him or start to get weird vibes. Are you meeting him at the Haven?" she asked.

"That's good advice and no, I'm not meeting him at the Haven. I don't want to risk seeing any clients or anyone else that I know. So, we are meeting at the Piano Bar across the street."

"Good idea. Have a good time and you call me if anything gets funky."

Joya loved Pam and her straightforwardness; there was never any pretense with her. "Will do," she laughed.

Zack texted Joya that he already arrived, had found a table for them and looked forward to seeing her. She replied to his text that she was also arriving as she crossed the street to enter the restaurant. She scanned the restaurant for him, but saw no one that resembled the photo burned in her memory from looking at it for the past month. He smiled as he approached her. "Hi, Joya. I'm Zack," he introduced himself. Joya looked at the short man who said that he was Zack. *You can't be Zack. Zack is six-two with a full head of hair. And a mustache.* The man standing before her was just a couple inches taller than her, with no facial hair and bald in the top. "Zack?" she questioned.

Ignoring her surprise, he hugged her, and then put his arm around her waist to lead her to the table he'd reserved for the two of them. He pulled her chair out, and then took his chair after she was seated. "You are more beautiful than your picture," he beamed. *And you look NOTHING like yours! Ugh!*

"Thank you," Joya replied politely. It would be a long hour with Zack, and she was now grateful for Pamela's advice. She ordered a white wine spritzer, which she knew she could drink quickly without it having an effect on her. The conversation with Zack was interesting enough, but Joya felt that she had been duped by the photo and how he'd mis-represented himself in his profile. He admitted that it was a photo that he'd taken prior to the balding process. "A few years ago," he said. He didn't say why he lied about his height.

He was saying something about a concert and asking Joya if she would like to go with him when the floor fell out from under her. *No! It can't be!* She shouted in her head. She had not seen him in what seemed like a hundred years, but she recognized him instantly, and her heart stopped beating – remembering. He was with a woman – not his wife. She recognized how he looked at the woman and how he held her hand across the table. He had looked at her like that- once upon a time. She thought he only looked at her that way – no one else. He took both of the woman's hands in his – she missed his touch.

He looked up and saw her across the room. His smile faded, he reactively let go of the woman's hands and looked at Joya with longing. The woman, noticing the yearning look in his eyes that wasn't directed to her, turned and looked at Joya. Then, she turned her attention back to Keith, demanding to know what was going on and who Joya was.

COULD this evening get any worse?! Joya inwardly screamed.

Chapter 46

Joya stomped three blocks from the Piano Bar to the Haven. She needed a real drink. She followed Pam's advice and told Zack that she had to get to her other commitment. "What about the concert?" he asked. "I'd like to see you again."

"I'll call you," she said already headed for the door, leaving Zack perplexed by her sudden action. She had to get out of there. She couldn't believe that she saw Keith out with a woman that wasn't his wife. *And she is not even cute!* She was sure that he was cheating on his wife. She was mad at herself for even caring. And for feeling that she was the one being cheated on. Keith ran out behind her, calling out to her. She ignored him, walking as fast as she could towards the Waterfront Haven. She thought that she was over him and realized that maybe she wasn't when she felt the tear trickle down her cheek. She wiped it away before walking through the revolving door to enter the restaurant.

She was glad to find that it wasn't very busy in the bar area, and she was able to find an empty high-top bar table. Terri saw her come in and checked her computer to make sure that she didn't have a reservation. A waitress was already greeting her, ready to take her drink order.

Bryce didn't see her come in, but noticed her sitting alone, seemingly lost in her thoughts. He was reviewing some wine catalogs when he looked up and noticed her. Concerned by her look, he decided to check on her. She was aware of his approach, wishing that he would go the other way. *Not tonight! I don't feel like talking! Especially to the male species!* She cut, then rolled her eyes at Bryce and looked the other way.

The look she gave him almost made him retreat. "Whoa!" he said. "I haven't even said anything to you yet, and you are looking at me like I owe you some money!" he said laughing, hoping to lighten her mood. He got a laugh out of her, taking that as an invitation to sit across from her. "So, what has you looking like you want to fight somebody? And don't tell me 'nothing.' "

She took a deep breath. "I guess a cheater is just a cheater," she blurted out, surprised that she said it, and unaware that it would touch a pain point for Bryce. She noticed it right away, but misunderstood. "I'm sorry; hope I'm not treading on familiar territory," she accused, thinking that he, too had cheated on someone.

"Do you have a habit of jumping to conclusions and making judgments?" he asked instead of accusing. She was ashamed of herself and quickly apologized. She shut up to avoid further humiliation. "Feel like talking about it?" he asked.

"Do you?" she countered. "It sounds like you might have a story to tell." *I'm interested. And I don't want to talk about my drama tonight.*

It had been a while since he talked about it, but Bryce opened up to Joya about the love of his life; how he worked two jobs to prepare for their life together. They lived together and were planning to be married. She was in graduate school, so their schedules didn't permit them to see each other as much as she wanted, mostly because he worked so many hours. Two weeks before they were to be married, he came home early to surprise her, but was the one surprised by her banging some guy he didn't know on the living room floor. She tried to make it his fault by not being home, not paying enough attention to her, and not fulfilling her needs. She admitted that it wasn't the first time.

"It's as if she wanted me to catch her. Why do it at our apartment and in the living room?" he brooded, re-living the scene he walked upon a long time ago, but that still pained him.

Joya could truly empathize with the pain he must have felt then and still feeling now. "I'm so sorry," she offered.

"We were young – probably too young to be getting married anyway."

"Have you been in a relationship since then?" Joya asked.

"Nothing serious. I still work a lot, so I don't want to make the same mistake twice."

"Maybe you work to avoid being in a relationship?" Joya probed.

Wise woman you are. "Maybe," he answered.

After Bryce's candid share, Joya decided to tell him a little of what happened with her at the Piano Bar. Bryce roared with laughter when she told him about Zack. *She's funny*, he thought. His heart went out to her when she told him about Keith. She only shared with him that she saw a friend who she suspected was cheating on his wife, and it upset her. He knew there was more to it than that, but he didn't press Joya for more than she was willing to share.

He remembered the wine brochures that he was looking at earlier and decided to change the subject. They both could use a break from discussing incidents that transported them to places that neither of them wanted to be. "Have you ever been to the wineries on the Eastern Shore? I have to go up there next month to check out some new wines. Would you like to go? I could use another opinion during the tastings." He was hopeful that she would agree to go.

"You're a nice guy, but I think I'm going to take a break from dating."

"How about it's NOT a date? I'll be working, and you'll be helping me."

Joya thought about it for a few seconds. *I do like wine tasting. But, I'll drive myself.* "Okay, then. It's NOT a DATE. Give me the information and I'll meet you there. After wine-tasting, I'll stop at the Outlet Mall to do my other favorite thing – shopping," she said smiling, grateful for the positive mood shift.

Chapter 47

Joya hardly made it through the door when she dialed Alise's number to tell her about the dating debacle. Normally, the first call would be to Sam, but they didn't talk as much since she'd started dating Rich. Joya needed to talk to Alise about Zack, but would not divulge the details about Keith. Only Sam knew the details of that love saga.

Alise found the story about Zack hilarious. "Girl, that is too funny!" she said. "But, not unusual," she added.

"You haven't heard the worst part. He told me that he needs to have both of his knees replaced! His profile says that he is forty, but he looks and acts closer to fifty! I think he is looking for a nurse," Joya laughed.

"Seriously? Both knees!" Alise shouted. What are you supposed to do with him other than nurse him back to health?" she agreed with Joya.

"Don't give up, girl. Unfortunately, there are some men like Zack that misrepresent themselves – " Alise started, but Joya interrupted. "Don't you mean LIE? Let's call it what it is!"

"Okay...Okay! Zack lied. But, there are some good honest men online. Just give it another chance," Alise maintained.

Not me! I'm deleting my profile as soon as we hang up! Joya changed the subject, vowing to delete her profile and never date anyone online again once she finished talking to Alise, but the conversation stretched longer than anticipated. While still talking to Alise, Joya pulled her iPad from her purse and logged into the dating site in preparation to delete her profile. She was surprised to see a message in her inbox. Up to that point, she chatted live with Zack and a few others, but never received a message before. Curious, she opened it.

She was drawn to the profile photo right away of an older, dark thin man with mixed gray hair and gentle smile. His description indicated that his age is fifty-one, and he lives in Manhattan. *Hmm...that's a two hour trip on the train, and since he is older, he should be finished playing games of the heart,* Joya considered. She read further to learn that he'd never been married, has one daughter and works as an investment broker on Wall Street. Joya didn't particularly like New York, but the idea of long-distance dating appealed to her. *He sounds really smart.*

"Are you listening to me?" Alise asked loudly, snapping Joya back to their conversation. She chuckled, "I'm sorry! I was distracted by 'Jason,' Joya informed Alise.

"Jason? Who's Jason?" she demanded, confused.

"I was about to shut down my profile when I saw a message from him. He looks interesting." Joya read Jason's profile and his message to Alise. He wrote to Joya that he thought her profile was interesting, and he was looking for an independent woman like her; the fact of her being a business owner particularly interested him. Alise shrieked with excitement. "See! I told you! He sounds great, and the distance might be good for you. And just think of all of the exciting things you can do in New York! Answer him, girl!"

"I just did," Joya said beaming with excitement.

Chapter 48

During the week that passed since Joya met Zack and saw Keith, it was non-stop at work, Sam and David were ringing her phones off of the hook, and she thought that Zack might be stalking her. Her suspicion was confirmed when she saw him across the street as she walked out her office building for lunch. She was reading a text message from Sam on her phone when she heard him call her name. Looking up, she could not believe it. She waved and he ran across the street, putting his arm around her waist. She recoiled.

"Hey, lady! I've been calling you; you been busy, huh?" he asked smiling. Joya felt a little sorry for him when she noticed his limp and remembered his upcoming knee replacements. "Hi, Zack. Yes, I have been busy. I received your voice mail messages." *All five hundred of them.* She stopped walking so that she could look at him. "Look – Zack, it's not going to work out with us. I enjoyed talking to you, and you are one of the nicest guys I've ever met, but I decided to explore some other options," she said thinking of Jason.

He frowned his face and turned his right ear towards her like he has having trouble hearing her. "But, what about the concert? I already bought the tickets."

"Zack, I apologize, but I never told you that I would go with you to the concert," Joya said a matter-of-factly.

"YOU BITCH!" he yelled at her, drawing the attention of the passersby. *Did he just call me a BITCH?* Not believing her ears, she decided to walk away. He caught up with her and grabbed her arm. "Don't walk away from me when I'm talking to you!" he shouted. "Don't you know that I could snap your little ass?"

This caught the attention of a young man who recognized Joya. He didn't know her name, but knew that they worked in the same building. "Get your hands off of me," Joya said to Zack through gritted teeth. The young man ran over to Joya and Zack, and reactively removed Zack's grip from Joya's arm and separated them with his body. He towered over Zack, was built like a wrestler and not to be challenged physically. "Move on, man," he said to Zack in a quiet, but threatening voice. Zack retreated without a word, not even looking back at Joya.

"Are you okay," he asked Joya. Embarrassed, she answered her rescuer, "Yes, I'm fine. Thank you so much. I'm so embarrassed, but I'm glad you walked up when you did. That guy is crazy." Wanting to thank him more, she asked, "We work in the same building, correct?" He confirmed, introducing himself, "Yes. I recognized you. I'm John. I work at the bank on the first floor."

"John, I'm Joya. I'm sorry that happened, but thank you again," she said ready to move beyond the incident and making a mental note to send John a thank-you note with a gift to show her appreciation.

Chapter 49

She no longer had an appetite and still shaken, Joya returned to her office. Although it was embarrassing, she was telling Pam about the confrontation with Zack, when Sam called, yet again. It had been a while since they'd talked, or hung out. Joya purposely avoided answering Sam's phone calls since Sam rarely answered her calls anymore. After all that was happening with her lately, she welcomed the opportunity to release it all with her best friend.

She filled Sam in on what transpired on the street with Zack. Sam listened intently, realizing that she was missing a lot of what was going on with Joya. She missed talking to her every day and vowed to correct that. She was so focused on her new relationship with Rich, but she had to remember the importance of her other relationships – with her family and friends. She invited Joya to meet her for dinner that evening. Joya accepted, looking forward to it especially since she had missed lunch, and also eager to spend time with Sam.

Joya drove her car out of the parking garage precisely at five-thirty, anxious to meet Sam at six o'clock at a new restaurant located downtown D.C. that she discovered with Rich. She was glad for a change of scenery and would be traveling against the rush hour traffic driving into the city. She shivered at the thought of her previous encounter with Zack and was second-guessing her communication with Jason when her cell phone buzzed a notification from the dating site. As if he read her mind, Jason sent her an instant message just to say 'Hi' and asked how her day was going. She ignored it.

Sam was waiting for Joya when she arrived at the restaurant right on time. They hugged like they had not seen each other in years because that's how it felt for both of them. They rarely had gone more than two or three days without communication. That was pre-Rich. Joya complimented Sam on how great she looked but thought she might have picked up a few pounds since she last saw her at the birthday/girlfriends celebration. She was careful not to mention it considering it could be her imagination or the fact that she had not seen her in a while.

After they placed their drink orders, Sam immediately probed Joya for the details about Zack which led to the 'Keith sighting', as Joya dubbed it. Sam skipped the details of Zack, for a moment, to address seeing Keith. "Why do you even care that he was out cheating on his wife? I know how you felt about him, but you knew back then that he had the potential to cheat." Sam didn't mince her words.

The words stung Joya, but she appreciated Sam's perspective. She was always able to be transparent with Sam and confessed, "I was mad or maybe jealous that he was with her, holding her hand, laughing with her... I felt like he was cheating o on me, I guess."

"Ahhh! So that's it. I thought you were over him? Joya, you need to let it go. He is married, and now you've confirmed that he is a CHEATER. Move on, girl. Let's talk about Zack. Do you feel safe?"

"I'm not sure," Joya answered honestly. I surely will be extra cautious for a while. At least he doesn't know where I live, but his knowing where I work is a little unnerving."

This is serious, Sam knew. "I think you should file a protective order. That way, he has to stay away. I'll help you."

"Do you think I should? Is it that serious?"

"Hell yeah! It's that serious! I would rather you play it safe."

She knew she wouldn't win the argument, so she agreed and reluctantly told her about Jason; she was curious about her perspective.

"I would say take it slow with him. I think it's a positive that it will be long distance dating; that would make it hard for him to stalk you," she said partially joking. "But, I do like that he works as an investment broker; considering that's true, he has to submit to periodic background and credit checks. Also, his reputation is important in his line of work, and I doubt that he would jeopardize his job. Lastly, I like that he is older and has a grown child. He is probably more serious about dating someone like you."

Joya exhaled, "I agree," she said, relieved.

"But – I think that you should get to know him here before you go traipsing off to New York. If he is serious about dating you, he will come to you. Make sure that he stays in a hotel and not in your home," Sam warned before finishing.

"I hear you. He says that he has business in D.C. often, so that would give us an opportunity to get to know each other when he is in town. Not to worry – I will go very slowly with him."

"So, tell me what's going on with you and Rich," Joya prompted, ready to hear all about the love interest apparently rocking her best friend's world.

Chapter 50

Sam beamed when she expressed her excitement about her relationship with Rich to Joya. "We share so many common interests: music, art, and travel; we're planning a trip to Rome, by the way. We are having so much fun together. We can talk about everything and he just gets me." She paused, wondering if she should continue. Joya was her best friend, so she decided to go for it. "Guess what?" she asked, not waiting for Joya to respond. "He LOVES chubby women! I don't have to worry about him being judgmental about how much I eat when we go out, AND he cooks for me!"

Ahh...that explains the weight gain. "He sounds absolutely wonderful. I'm glad that you have someone in your life that makes you happy. You are glowing!" Joya teased. "But, I have to ask as your friend – you worked so hard to lose the weight; you mentioned how great you felt, and you look fabulous. You don't want to gain the weight back do you?" Joya asked concerned. Sam's weight loss had been an arduous journey, and she didn't want to see her lose the time and energy she'd invested. There was also health issues associated with obesity to consider.

"No, I don't plan to go back to where I was before I was able to shop off the rack. I have way too many St. John Knits, and they fit my body perfectly," she laughed. "It's just good to know that he accepts me the way that I am and if I was bigger, it would be okay with him."

"Just be careful," Joya cautioned.

"There is one thing about him that does concern me."

"What is it?" Joya asked, slightly worried.

"He wants to get married. I am not interested in marrying him or anyone else. And you know that I don't do the 'mommy' thing. He has a teenaged daughter."

Shocked by the newsflash of Rich wanting to marry Sam, Joya took a drink of her Sangria and thought for a moment. "You haven't been dating that long. He has already raised the subject of marriage? What did you say?"

"I haven't said anything definitive, but I'm not marrying him or anyone else."

"What are you going to do? Do you love him?"

"I care for him, but I wouldn't say that I love him. I enjoy him. I appreciate him. What am I going to do? I'm going to enjoy the relationship for as long as I can. But, I can't see myself married to anyone."

Joya was puzzled. This was a side of Sam that was unfamiliar to her. "So, why string him along, knowing that he wants more of a commitment than you obviously do? I don't understand," she said, hoping that she wasn't offensive.

"I made it clear to him from the beginning that I was not looking to get married," she reported. "I like where we are, and I'm not interested, nor do I plan to see anyone else while we have our relationship, but I do not want to get married."

"Wow. I still don't understand, but okay," was all that Joya manage to say in response to Sam's revelation. She said a silent prayer that all would work out for her and Rich, and she had one more important matter to discuss with Sam while she had her attention.

"One more thing, Sam – I know that you are still somewhat in the honeymoon phase with Rich, am I'm so glad that you are in a meaningful relationship with someone that obviously cares for you, but don't forget your other relationships. I know that our friendship doesn't compare to being with the man that you care for, but remember that we also need to stay in touch and just be present for each other."

Sam totally understood where Joya was coming from, but made light of it, responding, "You miss me, don't you"? They both laughed.

"Yes, I do," Joya responded honestly. They pushed the jokes aside and promised each other to preserve the invisible, yet tangible thread that united them in loyal friendship.

Chapter 51

Joya struggled with whether or not to continue with Jason. So, far they had not met in person, but they both enjoyed the conversation with each other and wanted very much to meet. He was easy to talk to, therefore Joya disclosed to him the reason for her trepidation.

"I'm so sorry to hear that, Joya," Jason said referring to the incident with Zack that Joya told him about. "I'll tell you what. You know about six degrees of separation, right?" he asked.

"Of course," Joya responded, not sure where he was going, but definitely interested.

"Well, since I do a lot of business in D.C., I'm willing to bet that we both know some of the same people. I'll start naming some of my friends and business associates and let me know when you hear a familiar name. That might make you feel better about me if you know someone who also knows me. How does that sound?" he asked, wanting Joya to be comfortable. She agreed.

Jason started naming people that he thought might travel in the same circles as Joya. When he got to the eighth name, Joya yelled, "Bingo!" She was thrilled to hear Jason name a married couple, the Turners, also business owners that she knew and often saw at the County Chamber of Commerce meetings.

"I love them!" she beamed. "They have a really good non-profit youth program here in the county."

"Yes, I know. I help them from time-to-time when they need someone to do financial workshops for the kids. I'm doing one for them in the Spring."

Excited, Joya suggested, "That's great! Maybe we can meet in person when you are here for the workshop?"

"That won't be until May. I was hoping that we could get together before then?" he asked, hopeful.

Joya thought for a moment. "I guess we could do that. Would you be willing to come here?" she asked.

"Absolutely. Let's make plans," he said, glad that Joya was feeling more comfortable. He added, "I'll come down on the Acela; I just need you to recommend a nearby hotel." He decided to assuage any additional concerns that Joya might have.

Relieved, "Sure, Jason. That sounds good," she said. "Thanks for understanding – and for making me feel more comfortable."

"It's important that we both feel comfortable. I feel good about you, and I want you to feel the same."

They made plans for Jason to travel to D.C. in the next three weeks. It would be April, so the worst of the weather should be behind them. Joya had a renewed excitement and was looking forward to meeting Jason.

After they confirmed the date to meet in person, they talked for another hour before Joya noticed the time. She never stayed on the phone with anyone for that long – not since Keith.

Chapter 52

Joya moved with more pep in her step, and everyone noticed her heightened mood. She talked to Jason every evening after work. They could talk about anything and everything. She enjoyed hearing him talk about his work, his daughter, and his interests. He loved to travel, mentioning several places that he would like to visit with Joya.

Pam noticed the drastic change in Joya's mood over the past several days and mentioned it to her. She was glad to hear that Joya met someone she liked, especially after the incident with Zack.

Joya was looking forward to her end of the day talk with Jason when her cell phone rang. Anticipating that it would be Jason, she excitedly picked it up to answer, noticing the name displayed on the screen. It was David.

What does he want? She realized that she had not returned his last few calls although it was unintentional. She was just on a high with Jason and not thinking about calling David back. She still liked David as a friend and didn't want to offend him, so she answered, thinking that it needed to be quick because she was eager to talk to Jason.

"Hey, David," she answered.

"Hey, lady. How are you?"

"I'm good. What's up?" she asked, wanting to get to the point.

"I've left you a few messages. Why didn't you return my calls? Everything okay?" he asked, genuinely concerned.

Joya was aware of how much David still cared about her, and she didn't want to disrespect his compassion. He was a good person; it just wasn't their time. "Yes, everything is fine. I apologize for not calling you back; it's just been busy."

"I need to tell you something; it's important. Can I come over?"

Worried, she asked, "Are you okay? Yes, you can come over. I'll be here."

"I'm fine; no worries. I'll see you in twenty minutes."

Joya was concerned about what David had to tell her, but she didn't want to miss her evening talk with Jason. She sent him a text letting him know that she had a late meeting and would call him later.

David arrived at Joya's right on time as promised. She heard his car pull into the driveway and was waiting at the door for him. He was glad to see her, but nervous about her reaction to his news. Despite his worry, he smiled at Joya as he walked through the front door, and leaned forward to kiss her on the cheek. She led him to the kitchen where they took their seats at the kitchen island.

"What's going on? Should I be worried?" she asked wanting to get right to the point. He reached for her hand; she could tell that he was nervous, but waited for him to respond. "I've been trying to tell you for a few weeks…I wasn't sure what you would say…but, Lynn and I finally split up. I moved out." He looked deeply into her eyes, "It's been a long time coming, but I'm hoping that it's not too late for us?" he asked.

Joya, now on an emotional rollercoaster, withdrew her hand from his, got up from her chair and walked to the other side of the island to put some distance between them. "I'm not sure what to say. Congratulations?" Curious, she asked, "When did you move out?"

David didn't expect her reaction. He had dreamed of Joya throwing her arms around him when she heard about his liberation. And then, he would finish what they started in the D.R.; he would make passionate love to her and become her man. All he wanted was to take care of her and love her.

"I moved out a few weeks ago. I didn't tell you before because you were planning your birthday, and then the weather got bad – it wasn't something that I wanted to tell you over the phone. I thought that your reaction would be different. I thought that you wanted us to be together, and the only reason you stopped seeing me was because of my situation."

"That was the reason, but a lot of time has passed since then; I'm not even sure what I want anymore…" she said, thinking of Jason. Although they had not met in person, she liked him so far and wanted to see where things would go with them.

"Joya, please give me a chance; give us a chance?" he pleaded.

"I don't know, David. I wanted us to be together, yes; but now...I'm just in a different place in my life."

Surprised by her answer, he asked if she would at least give it some thought. She agreed that she would think about it, but it would take some time.

He left feeling deflated and that he was at least a day late even if not a dollar short.

Chapter 53

Why am I so nervous? Joya paced the waiting area of the Amtrak station, checking her watch over and over. *Is the train late?* She was feeling flushed and knew she was stressing herself unnecessarily. Jason would soon be getting off of the six o' clock train to spend the weekend in D.C. She had been looking forward to it ever since they'd planned it, but now she was a nervous wreck. She wanted to calm down so that her color would return; she was sure that she was blushing red all over.

She took several deep breaths, and then she saw him walk towards her. He had a confident stride and was taller than she thought he would be, distinguished, professional and well-dressed. He smiled as soon as he recognized her, and she forgot about her anxiety. They hugged like they had always known each other, not like they were meeting for the first time.

"Hi, Jason. I'm glad you made it!" Joya said, returning his hug.

He looked directly into her eyes, "We finally meet," he said, sweetly. He slung his leather garment bag over his shoulder and grabbed Joya's hand with his free hand. "Lead the way," he said.

They talked non-stop from the moment they fell into step with each other to head to Joya's car and right through dinner. Joya selected a posh, upscale

Latin-American restaurant that provided the perfect blend of quietude and delectable menu choices. They were both so invigorated with the prospect of having intellectually stimulating conversation with each other, they didn't notice when the restaurant was almost empty. The server never rushed them, and checked on them often, but gave them the space he sensed was needed.

Jason was the first to notice the time and signaled for the check. Joya apologized, "I'm sorry. I didn't mean to keep you out this long after your trip. You're probably tired."

"Not too tired to have dessert and another glass of wine with you," he said as he grabbed her hand and led her to a dessert bar he knew of just a few blocks away on 19th Street. Joya liked his style and easy going manner. Neither of them was ready for the evening to end. They decided to share a fruit and nut dessert and a bottle of sparkling water. It was late, and she was careful not to over-imbibe on the first date and she still had to drive home after dropping Jason at the hotel.

They were both more comfortable and were enjoying each other. Jason picked up the last bite of the dessert and teased Joya, waving the fork-filled treat in front of her. She liked his flirting and flirted back with her eyes. "Oooh – with a look like that, you get the last bite," Jason said, moving the fork to her mouth. He was clumsy with the delivery and Joya was awkward on the receiving end, resulting in the fork nicking her lip.

"Oh! Joya! I'm so sorry! Are you okay?" He exclaimed, drawing attention from their server who came running over. Joya pulled the napkin away from her lip that immediately felt a little swollen, to see a small spot of blood. The sight of the blood alarmed Jason and the server more than Joya. "I'm okay – really," she muttered, placing the napkin back to her lip. She assured the server she was okay, but the restaurant management comped their dessert and water, not wanting any trouble. Jason planned to leave more than enough to cover their order, plus a sizeable tip for the server since it was clearly his fault.

Embarrassed, Joya suggested, "I think we should go; I don't want to draw any more attention." She was already out of her chair, so Jason jumped to help her. When they reached the street, Joya exhaled her relief. Jason squeezed her hand, "I feel awful. You must think I'm the clumsiest guy you ever met," he said, also embarrassed. "What can I do?"

Joya knew that he was ashamed and wanted to alleviate his concern. Since flirting had gotten them into the situation, maybe flirting would get them out, she thought. "Maybe you could kiss it to make it feel better?" she asked, looking at his dark, full, delicious lips.

"I can do that," he said, pulling her into his arms, gently kissing her lips, careful not to aggravate the bump that formed on the corner of her bottom lip. Joya smiled at him when he pulled away. "Thank you. I feel better already," she said leading the way to the car.

Chapter 54

The rest of the weekend was a whirlwind of delight that included a little Washington, D.C. historical sightseeing, lots of hand holding, food sharing and a romantic dinner on the Annapolis waterfront Sunday night. Jason was scheduled to leave on the first train Monday morning and wanted to evaluate Joya's desire for their relationship. He liked her a lot, wanted to see more of her and made it known to her.

"So, Miss Alexander," he began as he reached across the table to hold her hand. "What do you think about us so far?"

Joya didn't expect the question so soon, but she wanted to be honest. "I have to tell you, Jason, that I have had one of the best weekends of my life. I like how we click and that we can talk about everything. What are your thoughts?"

"Good, I'm glad that you feel that way; I feel the same. You are a breath of fresh air for me, and I think we have something here. I think that we are good for each other and the perfect compliment to each other. " He paused for Joya's reaction, and when she smiled, he continued, "I would like for us to see more of each other – exclusively."

Definitely not expecting that, Joya sipped her champagne. "Well – what do you think?" he asked.

The image of David flashed before her. *Don't mess this up, Joya! He's a good man – not playing games!* She had casually mentioned him to the Turners when she saw them at a county event. They couldn't say enough good things about him, which helped to ease her concerns. "I think that you are a good man for me – one that I've been looking for quite a while - and I'm fortunate that we met when we did. Yes, let's do this!" she said excited, raising her glass to toast their relationship.

They made plans for Jason to visit Joya again in two weeks since he would be on business travel the following week and into the weekend. He suggested that he stay at the hotel again until Joya was totally comfortable with their relationship; she agreed.

Jason massaged Joya's neck and shoulders while she drove from Annapolis back to his hotel. No one had ever done that for her before and she enjoyed the attention. She decided to follow him to his room; she wanted a little more time with him and a proper sendoff. He arranged for car service to transport him to the train station in the morning since he was leaving so early. He didn't want Joya to have to deal with Monday morning rush hour traffic.

She initiated the embrace, wrapping her arms around his waist. "I had the best weekend. I don't want you to go," she said looking up into his eyes.

"I had a great time, too. I'm going to miss you this week, but we'll talk on the phone and I'll be back in two weeks." He lowered his head to kiss her lips already healing from the very minor injury.

Joya thought he was still careful, suspecting that she might still be in pain. She pressed her lips to his to let him know she was okay and that she wanted him to kiss her without caution. *Kiss me like you mean it.* His kiss was the same.

There were no fireworks or movement of the earth for Joya, but she felt secure. She finally had a man of her own that was honest – not out to hurt her, and he didn't belong to another woman.

Thank you, God. Keep him safe, she prayed as she hugged him goodbye.

Chapter 55

Joya beamed as she walked into the salon. Naya noticed it immediately. "Hi, Joya. I'll be right with you," she said as she put the finishing touches on the customer in her chair.

Joya's phone buzzed. It was a text from Bryce reminding her about the Wine Tasting she agreed weeks ago to attend with him. It was this coming Saturday. Joya cringed when she read the text. She totally forgot, but she would not renege on her word. She felt a little uneasy about it since she was now in a relationship with Jason. But, since there was no romantic interest between her and Bryce, she was sure that it would be fine. She would make sure to tell Jason about it when she talked to him.

She was finishing up her confirmation text to Bryce when Naya approached her to lead her to the shampoo area. "You look great, Joya. What's been going on with you?" Naya asked.

"Girl, I think I finally found a man that I can have a decent relationship with," she blurted to Naya. She was bursting at the seams to share her joy.

"That is great! I'm so glad for you. Tell me about him," Naya urged.

Joya told her about how they met, his recent trip and that they have mutual business colleagues. Naya was aware from the conversation they had at Joya's birthday celebration how apprehensive she was about online dating and was glad to hear that she was experiencing a positive outcome.

"Knowing someone familiar with him must make you feel more secure, especially after 'Zack-Attack!' You haven't seen him anywhere, have you?" Naya asked, concerned. Joya told Naya about Zack right after it happened. Although she had followed Sam's advice to get the protective order and even though he had not risen his bald head since that day, she still looked over her shoulder.

"Right?" Joya laughed at Naya's appropriate moniker for Zack. "No, I haven't seen him, thank God. But, he might be somewhere laid up with his new knees," Joya said referring to the knee replacements he told her about.

Naya laughed with Joya about Zack, but wanted to hear more about Jason. "So, are you seeing him again this weekend?"

"I wish, but no. He is on business travel. But, we talk every day. He calls to say 'good morning' and we talk again every night usually until after midnight. I like him a lot," she gleamed, admitting her feelings to Naya.

"Finally! I've always said that you need a man that can appreciate you for the strong, unique woman that you are. Jason sounds like that man. Let me know when you plan to get married; I want to write a wedding song for you."

"Awww – that's so sweet, Naya. I would love that! We aren't there yet, but you know I'll give you a full report every two weeks!" Joya said.

"So, what are you doing this weekend since your man is on travel?"

'My man' – I like the sound of that, Joya thought, smiling up at Naya while she shampooed her hair. "I'm going to a winery on the Eastern Shore. I'm meeting a bartender there from the Waterfront Haven restaurant. He has to go up there to try some new wines, and he asked me to go before I met Jason, but it's not a date. He sent me a text message a few minutes ago to remind me."

Naya was inquisitive, but never judgmental. "So, if it's not a date, what is it?"

Joya pondered for a moment before answering, "I think he asked me because I'm a regular customer, and we've been talking a lot lately when I'm there alone."

"Hmmm. He could be interested in you. It's good to have options," she added matter-of-factly, which made Joya think.

Bryce interested in me? Naw...

Chapter 56

When Joya arrived at the Easton Winery, Bryce was already there. She had no idea what kind of car he would be driving, but she saw him standing on the porch of the main house talking to who she assumed was their guide for the visit. Bryce smiled when he saw her walk towards them.

"Here she is now," he informed the lady standing opposite him.

"Hey, Joya. I'd like you to meet the owner of this fabulous winery – Joanna. Joanna, this is one of Waterfront Haven's best customers – Joya."

Joanna extended her hand to Joya with a welcoming smile, "Welcome, Joya. Any friend of Bryce's is a friend of ours here at Easton Winery."

"Thank you, Joanna. It's nice to meet you. Your property is beautiful," Joya complimented the lady who was about her height. Joya liked her casual, yet professional and respectful demeanor that made her feel right at home in her vineyard. "We have a lot of new wines for you two to taste – follow me," she invited. Bryce placed his hand at the small of Joya's back guiding her in front of him and directly behind Joanna to walk into the Tasting Room. Joanna put on quite a show, pouring samples of several red and white wines, both sweet and dry, paired with a variety of fruit, meat, and cheeses.

After the lavish sampling, Joya browsed the Gift Shop while Bryce and Joanna conducted their business. They caught up with her near the front of the store where was admiring the unique handmade jewelry and wine stoppers. She turned when Joanna touched her arm and handed her a gift bag. "This is for you," she said, "as a first-time customer. I hope that you will come back sometime," she said with a smile.

Joya accepted the tall gift bag that nestled a bottle of sweet red that she liked. "I noticed that you seemed to like this one the best, so I wanted you to go home with a bottle," Joanna informed her.

"That is really sweet – thank you so much," Joya said drawing Joanna into a friendly hug. "I didn't expect it; it's a nice surprise. I'll share it with my boyfriend when he comes to visit next weekend. Maybe we will drive up; he would love it!" Joanna shot a glance to Bryce that wasn't returned. She assumed that Bryce and Joya were a couple since he had always come alone in the past. *So much for assuming,* she thought.

Boyfriend? Joya's comment took Bryce by surprise, but he didn't show it outwardly. He thanked Joanna again, hugged her goodbye and led Joya outside to the parking lot.

Aware of the awkward silence, Joya turned to Bryce, "Thanks for inviting me today. I really enjoyed it. Which wines did you select for the restaurant?" she asked as they walked towards her car.

"I'm glad that you came," he said then ran down the list of wines he'd selected. "So, your friend will be in town next weekend? You should bring him to the restaurant. We should have the first shipment of new wines by then. I'd like to meet the man that has your heart," he teased.

"Maybe I will," she said. "We are still new, so he doesn't have my heart yet. But, I do like him," she added, not sure why. *Why did I just say that? Bryce doesn't care how I feel about Jason.*

Bryce wanted to size up Joya's new dating interest, although he wasn't sure if his curiosity came from a place of brotherly protection or some other place where he had not been in quite a while.

Chapter 57

New York had not been one of Joya's favorite places, but she was excited about experiencing it with Jason. After a few more weeks of him traveling to the D.C. area to visit Joya, he bought her a train ticket to visit him in New York. In between visits, they still talked every morning and night and he sent her favorite purple, sometimes red, roses to her office. She now looked forward to getting her mail at home because there would often be a sentimental card from Jason to let her know that he was thinking about her.

She loved the attention he was showing her, she was comfortable with him and eagerly anticipated the trip to New York. He was waiting for her when she arrived at Penn Station on Friday evening, enfolded her in his arms and led her to the town car waiting for them outside. They sat close, holding hands and talking non-stop for the entire ride to Jason's apartment.

She was awestruck at his Penthouse apartment decorated in rich mahogany and beige tones, and magnificent view of the Manhattan skyline. He had a bottle of champagne on ice and popped the cork to welcome Joya to his little corner of the world for the first time.

They sat on the sofa, talking, sipping champagne and enjoying the view. "We have dinner reservations in thirty minutes," Jason informed Joya. "Do you mind walking? It's only a few blocks, but we can get a car if you want."

"I would love to walk," Joya answered. "I'm looking forward to experiencing New York with you!" she said enthusiastically.

"Good, because I plan to spoil you," he said kissing her lightly on the lips.

Spoil me! Joya welcomed the idea of being spoiled by her man.

True to his word, Jason showed her the best that Manhattan had to offer, starting with dinner at this favorite Italian restaurant on Friday, shopping on Fifth Avenue on Saturday, dinner and Broadway play on Saturday night and brunch with his parents on Sunday after church. Joya and Jason's parents, Wallace and Agnes, fell in love instantly.

A delightful couple in their seventies, Joya thought that Jason looked more like his dad, but also recognized qualities of his mother in his personality. Agnes seemed to be more talkative while Wallace was more pensive. An only child, Jason had come from good stock, Joya concluded. After they enjoyed a delectable brunch and they were all full, Joya and Jason stood with Wallace and Agnes while they waited for their car to pull around to pick them up. Agnes turned to face Joya so that she had her back to the men who were engaged in a separate conversation about sports. She took her hand when she said, "You are a beautiful girl, Joya. Thank you for making my son happy. I've never seen him so alive."

Chapter 58

It had been a full weekend, and Joya planned to leave on the first train back to D.C. in the morning. Brunch with Jason's parents had ended well into the late afternoon, and it was early evening by the time she and Jason leisurely walked through the park and back to his apartment. The July heat and humidity of the city didn't faze her as long as she was with her man.

He massaged her feet as they relaxed on the sofa. "So, Miss Alexander – how was your weekend in New York City?" he asked looking deeply into her eyes. He loved having her around and hoped that she felt the same about him. He was also glad that his parents liked her and she seemed comfortable with them. It was important to him that his parents approve of her. They never liked his daughter's mother, always cordial towards her, but never warm and friendly.

"Oh, that feels so good," she said referring to her foot massage. "I have enjoyed my first weekend with you in your city, Mr. White," she said leaning forward to kiss his cheek. He pushed her foot aside and pulled her into his arms, kissing her tenderly. His kiss still didn't move Joya, but she admired and appreciated the man behind the kiss and who he had shown her that he was. She returned his kiss, placing her hand on his face, drawing him closer.

He rested his forehead on Joya's, saying, "I was a lost soul before you came into my life. Thank you," he said. Joya heard the emotion in his voice. She looked directly into his eyes, answering, "We saved each other. Thank YOU."

He hugged her tightly. She whispered in his ear, "Are you afraid of falling in love?"

"With you? Not at all. Truthfully, I fell in love with you weeks ago," he confessed.

"I love you, too," Joya whispered and decided it was time to consummate their feelings for each other. She stretched out onto the sofa and pulled him on top of her. He was breathing hard, kissing her neck and unbuttoning her blouse. She began to slowly unbutton his shirt. She liked how his full, soft lips felt on her neck, and she moaned to let him know she enjoyed it.

She reached for his belt to unfasten it; he raised his waist to allow her to reach it. She expertly unbuckled it, and then unzipped his pants so that she could push them down. He lowered himself back on top of Joya. She massaged his butt and felt the tiny hairs respond. With that, she raised her legs, caught his underwear between her toes and pushed them down. He was surprised that she could do that with her feet, and it made him chuckle. "Wow - you got skills," he said releasing his pants and boxers to the floor. Joya helped him to unzip her dress and remove her panties.

"I want you, Jason," Joya whispered as she looked into his eyes. "I've waited a long time for a man like you."

"I want you, too, Joya. I love you so much," he moaned. "I want to be the only man ever to touch you this way again," he said sweetly.

He said the right words with the right amount of passion, but Joya didn't feel his passion physically. They were touching flesh-to-flesh, but Joya didn't feel his desire for her. She adjusted herself under him so that she could make closer contact - still nothing. He was aware of what she was doing, and he rolled off of her.

Not understanding at all, she rolled her body towards him, taking his face into her hands. "What's wrong, baby?" she asked, confused.

"I want you so badly, Joya. I don't know why I can't," he said turning away embarrassed and frustrated. This was a first for Joya. She had never been with a man who could not perform. She had to remember that Jason is older at age fifty-one, than any man she had ever been with.

She turned his face back towards her, but he wouldn't open his eyes. "Look at me," she softly requested. When he opened his eyes, she made it clear to him that she was not going to let this incident dictate their relationship. "I love you. My love does not command or make demands. We will figure this out. It doesn't change how I feel about you." He didn't respond and it worried Joya.

"Okay?" she appealed to him to answer. He wrapped his arms around her and held her tightly. He kissed her forehead, saying, "Thank you, sweetheart. I'll make this up to you – I promise."

Chapter 59

Summer was a blur and it was the beginning of Fall before Joya and Sam could connect with each other in person, but they'd kept their pact of talking every few days. Sam and Rich were still a couple and Joya and Jason were getting closer, even indirectly discussing the prospect of taking their relationship to the next level – marriage. Sam and Joya had a lot to catch each other up on and Joya didn't want to be restricted to time in a restaurant, so she invited Sam over on Sunday afternoon. Jason was on business travel and Joya welcomed the opportunity to catch up on personal stuff and time with her best friend.

They sat in Joya's morning room, enjoying the scenery of the changing colors brought on by the seasonal change while they sipped green tea and ate smoked salmon salad that Joya prepared. Joya noticed that Sam's weight was still going in the wrong direction, but she was careful not to mention it.

"Catch me up on you and 'Mr. Wonderful,' " Joya said referring to Rich. "How was your trip to Rome?"

"Girl, it was the trip I've always dreamed of. We had the best time! And the restaurants – we ate the best food!" Sam exclaimed. *Yeah I can see that*, Joya secretly thought.

"That's great, Sam. I'm so happy for you," Joya responded, genuinely happy for her friend.

"We travel well together. We are planning a trip to Morocco for the holidays."

"Really?" Joya asked, surprised. "So, things sound good; no more conversation about marriage?"

"We had a talk about it. I made it clear to him – again – that I am not interested in marriage. He says that he is okay with it."

Suspicious, Joya probed, "Suppose he changes his mind later?"

"Then he changes his mind. I won't be changing mine," Sam answered straightforwardly. "I've been honest with him about it, so if he changes his mind or doesn't understand, it's not because he has not been informed."

"What about you? How are things with you and Jason," she asked wanting to know, but also ready to shift the conversation away from Rich and marriage. It was an irritating subject that she wanted to avoid at all times.

"Well, we are talking about a future together. We haven't actually said the word, 'marriage', but he appears to be going that way," Joya informed Sam.

"What?! That's great!" Sam shouted. Joya didn't understand why Sam could be so excited for her to get married, but was so against it for herself and she decided to ask her.

"How come you are so excited about me getting married - and it's not for sure yet - but repulsed by the thought of getting married yourself?"

"It's simple: because you WANT to be married and I DON'T!" Sam shouted, now showing her irritation with Joya.

"Okay, Okay! I got it! I won't ask you again." She continued by telling Sam how Jason spoiled her when he came to visit her and when she visited him in New York and all the little things he did in between as well as her love affair with his parents.

"Aww – he sounds so sweet," Sam said. "That is the difference in a mature man and one that is still playing games or doesn't know what he wants – like David. What's up with him? I haven't heard you mention him in a while and that's a good thing." Joya brought Sam up-to-speed on David's separation and the last conversation they'd had.

"Seriously? He thought that you would just jump into his arms after he took his sweet time to fix his situation? I'm so glad that you and Jason were already starting to see each other. Otherwise, you probably would've fallen for it."

"Who knows what would have happened?" she reminisced of her night of passion with David in the D.R. Sam detected that Joya had drifted to another place.

"What's that look about?" Sam asked.

She decided to be honest, "Just thinking about how we almost got busy when we were in the D.R.," she answered.

"Huh? If Jason is rocking your world like he's supposed to, you shouldn't be thinking about it."

Joya didn't respond, which prompted Sam to ask, "He is rocking your world, isn't he?"

Joya sipped her tea before answering, "Not really. I'm not sure if he has some type of medical issue or what's happening. He's been to the doctor, but for some reason he cannot take anything for erectile dysfunction." Joya was relieved to discuss this with Sam; she was confident that she would keep it confidential. She had not discussed it with anyone else, not even Mona who is a nurse.

"So, am I to understand that you have not had sexual intercourse in the many months that you've been seeing him?"

Slightly embarrassed, she answered, "You make it sound so clinical. And, to answer your question – no, not really. He puts forth a considerable effort to please me, but it's not enough. I want to please him too, but I don't know what to do for him. Nothing arouses him. I thought it was me, that I couldn't turn him on, but he denies that. He seems hurt when I ask him if I'm the problem. I only want to know what I could do to stimulate him. I've tried everything..." Joya shook her head.

Sam had to ask, "Would you be happy in a sex-less marriage?"

"I love Jason and he loves me. I admire his intelligence and I appreciate the man that he is and how he treats me. Do I want to be in a sex-less marriage? No. We are intimate, just not 'sexual intercourse' intimate. But, I'm willing to make that sacrifice for Jason because of everything else that he brings to the relationship; qualities that I've always wanted, but couldn't find."

There must be more to Jason's non-performance, Sam was thinking. She was thinking that he might be gay or have a health issue that he was not being honest about.

Whatever the reason, Sam didn't like it. Joya always sacrificed herself in her relationships and this seemed to have 'tragedy' written all over it.

"Let's plan a dinner for the four of us the next time he's in town. I'd like to meet my future brother-in-law," Sam teased.

I need to meet this man before Joya does something that she will regret. Will she ever learn?

Chapter 60

Joya was surprised to see Bryce in the First Class car on the train to New York when she boarded. He had boarded at the earlier stop in Maryland. Joya lived closer to that stop also, but she liked to leave from the D.C. station because there was a train to and from New York Penn Station every hour. Bryce was surprised when he looked up from his magazine and saw Joya heading towards him.

"Hey! What a surprise. Are you traveling alone?" he asked, hoping that she was.

"Hey there, friend," she returned the greeting. "Are you heading to New York?"

"Yes. Would you like to join me?" he invited her to sit with him, already standing to help her place her garment bag overhead. He stepped aside to let her sit next to the window. She accepted his invitation, welcoming the opportunity to have someone to talk to. She usually read or talked to Jason or Alise on her cell on the ride up, but she had not talked to Bryce in a while. She had been to the Haven a few times since their Wine Tasting trip, but was usually entertaining clients, not having time for an extended conversation with Bryce.

After she took her seat, he helped her out of her leather coat. It was the first week of December and she would need that and more in New York this time of year, he thought. "Are you traveling for business?" he asked, closing the magazine he had been reading.

"I'm going up to see, Jason, my boyfriend," she answered.

"Oh. I remember you mentioning him when we were at the winery, but I didn't realize he lived in New York."

"Yep. It makes for an interesting relationship having to travel back and forth, but I've come to like New York. He lives in Manhattan and we enjoy it. Are you going up to visit friends or family?" she asked.

"I have friends in Manhattan as well; a couple of buddies from college. I'm going up to get a jump on my Christmas shopping and see a basketball game; you know, just hanging out," he said.

"Sounds like fun," Joya smiled. "Who's watching the bar at the Haven while you're away?" she joked.

Who's watching the bar? Bryce wasn't sure how to answer, but he told Joya that it was under control. "What do you and Jason have planned for the weekend? The Christmas tree is being lit at Rockefeller Center this weekend."

"I know!" Joya said excited. "And the stores on Fifth Avenue unveil their holiday windows. I can't wait. I haven't been to New York for the holidays since I was a kid. My parents would bring my sister and me up for the weekend during the holidays so that we could see the store windows. We couldn't afford to shop Fifth Avenue, but it was fun seeing all of the decorations and we LOVED Macy's at Christmas!"

Bryce enjoyed her excitement. "We grew up in Philadelphia, so we would take the train and spend the whole day, too. My sister and I even ice-skated at the Rockefeller Center Rink while my parents watched," he said with fond remembrance. "I think every kid should experience New York during the holidays."

He is such a nice guy, Joya thought. He deserves a decent woman. If he had one, she surely would be traveling with him. Joya was curious, "Are you seeing any one?" she asked. She remembered the conversation they had about his heartbreak.

"How did we jump from holiday nostalgia in New York to my love life? But, as I recall, you like to jump around, especially to conclusions," he joked. She laughed with him. "No, I'm not seeing anyone," he finally answered.

"That's too bad, because I see that you would make a special lady very happy. You have a lot to offer."

Where is this coming from? Bryce thought. "You think so?"

"I do," Joya said, and then changed the subject; she wasn't sure why she had taken them down that tract. They talked more about the holidays, traditions and shopping and before they realized that two hours had passed, they were pulling into Penn Station.

"So, I'll see you back on our side of town, Bryce. I'm sure that I'll be at the Haven in the next week or so," Joya said gathering her belongings. Bryce reached overhead to retrieve her garment bag and handed it to her.

"I'll be there. It's our busiest time, of course. We are closed for a private party on New Year's Eve, but we are having a party for our staff on the thirtieth. You should come by," Bryce suggested as they made their way from the train to the street level. "Bring Jason, if he's in town." *I hope he won't be in town.*

"Thanks for the invite. I'm not sure what we are doing for New Year's, but I'll let him know. Enjoy your weekend," she said as she scrolled through her phone to order an Uber car. Jason was still at work and he had given her a key to his apartment weeks ago. She planned to get settled, and then pick up dinner for them at the restaurant in his building.

Bryce sat in the back seat of the taxi that he'd hailed, wondering what type of guy Jason was.

And why he even cared.

He wouldn't care.

Chapter 61

"That's the third time they've gone around," Jason said referring to the young couple skating on the ice at Rockefeller Center. "Come on... you can do it," he encouraged the young man from afar, although he could not be heard. Joya laughed at Jason's enthusiasm for the couple. It was obvious to everyone that he was planning to propose to the young lady skating with him. She had her arm looped through his as he led her around the rink once more while he recorded their revolutions via cell phone mounted on a selfie stick.

He finally stopped in front of the Christmas tree that had been ceremoniously lit earlier that evening. He clumsily went down on one knee, and pulled out a ring with his free hand. Although Joya and Jason were unable to hear his exact words, they knew he was asking the young lady to marry him. She nodded and helped him place the ring on her finger. Everyone applauded, including Joya and Jason, maybe especially Jason which surprised Joya. He yelled out, 'Yes!' as soon as the young lady nodded her head indicating she accepted the proposal.

They stood in the brilliance of the multi-colored lights of the famous tree watching the skaters. Jason had Joya wrapped in his arms to help keep her warm. It was the first time that he enjoyed the splendor of the holidays with a woman that he cared about. He brought his daughter every year when she was a teenager and watched while she skated with her friends, but it was magical sharing the holiday joy with Joya - the woman he loved. He was sure that she loved him, too, in spite of his physical problem. He was still working on it...he had stopped taking his meds, despite warning from Dr. Porter, but there was no improvement. He had to figure out something else.

"Aren't you quite the cheering squad for the young lovers!" Joya joked, looking back at him over her shoulder.

"I knew he could do it," he laughed. He turned her around to face him, his arms still wrapped around her. She wrapped her arms around him, oblivious to the biting cold, enjoying the night and how good she felt with him.

"If they love each other half as much as we do, they will be happy forever," he said kissing her lips. "I agree," Joya said returning his kiss.

"What would you have said had that been us out there?" he asked.

"First of all, that wouldn't be us on the ice!" She punched his shoulder.

"Come on! You know what I mean. Seriously, if I ask you, would you say 'yes?' " he asked, concerned about her response.

"IF you ever ask me, I would definitely say 'Yes.' " Thrilled, he picked her up and twirled her around.

When he placed her feet back on the ground, he bent forward to kiss her again.

"Wait! What just happened?" Joya asked laughing. "Did you just propose to me?"

"That was a pre-proposal. I just wanted to make sure that you will say 'Yes' when I do officially propose."

That is so romantic, Joya thought as she stood on her toes to accept his kiss. *I look forward to being your wife.*

Chapter 62

Joya was reluctant to attend the annual WalkerSinclair Holiday Party as she had every year. David would surely be there since he works for the law firm. She had not heard from him since the night he told her about his separation from his wife, Lynn.

He saw her when she entered the room. His heart still melted whenever he saw her. He hoped that he would have heard from her by now, but was also wanted to grant her the time and space she requested. He had an excuse tonight to approach her. He needed to be a good host to the guests that had been invited to the holiday party and Joya was one of those guests.

She saw him walk towards her which put her nerves on edge. She expected to see him, but hoped to be in conversation with others so as to avoid him. *Here he comes,* she thought. She gave him her best professional smile, "Hi, David. Good to see you," she said. He pulled her into a hug that she didn't expect. It was cordial and not intimate, but still made her uncomfortable.

"Hi, Joya. I'm so glad that you came," David said, looking at her longingly.

"I haven't missed one of WalkerSinclair's Holiday parties since I moved into the building," she said, remembering that was how they'd originally met.

"Let me get you a drink," he offered. "No thanks," she declined. "I see some folks that I need to talk to you. I'll catch up with you later," she stated while walking away.

Sam and Rich came in within a few minutes of Joya's arrival, which provided the buffer she needed to avoid David. He was aware of Sam's opinion of him, so he intentionally avoided a conversation with her after his initial welcome to her and Rich when they arrived. He also knew that Joya was purposely avoiding him, but when he saw a moment of opportunity, he decided to take advantage of it. Joya was walking towards the door to leave. He set his drink down and rapidly moved in her direction.

"Joya, can we talk for a minute?" he pleaded.

"David, I really have to go."

He touched her shoulder, gently not threatening. "Have you thought about what we talked about? I just want to know. "

Joya didn't want to talk to David at the holiday party, but since he insisted on an answer, she gave it to him. "I'm involved with someone and it's serious. We are talking about the possibility of marriage. There is no future for us, David. I appreciate your friendship and hope that we can continue to be friends."

"I understand. Thanks for telling me." She thanked him for a nice holiday party and walked through the door to leave.

"Joya –" David called out to her. She turned to see what he wanted.

"Good luck to you both." He still loved her wanted the best for her, even if that meant being with someone else.

Chapter 63

Something was off, but Joya couldn't quite put her finger on it. It was only last week that Jason was kissing her at Rockefeller Center and asking her if she would consider spending the rest of their lives together. She noticed it as soon as she saw him walking towards her car when she picked him up at the train station the very next Friday evening. He didn't have the usual pep in his step; he was sluggish instead with a scowled expression that she didn't recognize . Joya wrote it off as fatigue since he had been working and traveling more so than usual to make the year-end financial goals of the brokerage firm.

They enjoyed dinner at one of their favorite restaurants downtown on Friday night, but he was extremely restless and didn't sleep, which meant that Joya also was awake through the night. She turned over to hug him, kissing his back lightly. She thought it was her imagination or a reflex when he moved her hand from his chest when she softly caressed his firm pects. It wasn't meant to be anything other than a gesture of affection. Joya had all but given up on trying to turn him on, accepted their emotional love for each other and prayed that his 'situation' would soon correct itself.

When he moved her hand, she was startled. "Are you okay?" she whispered.

He exhaled in exasperation, "I'm fine. I just can't sleep," he muttered and rolled out of bed.

"What's wrong? Do you feel okay?" Joya asked, sitting up and turning on the light.

"Joya, I'm fine," he snapped. "Go back to sleep. I'm going downstairs to read for a while."

Excuse me? Joya thought, but didn't say anything as she watched him walk out of the bedroom. She turned off the light, but didn't go back to sleep. He had never spoken to her in that tone and it angered her, but mostly concerned her. But, she would give him some space and hope that he would be in a better mood when they joined Sam and Rich for dinner on Saturday evening.

After breakfast, Jason appeared to be in a better mood and said that he wanted to get some work done before going out to dinner. Joya left him sitting with his laptop in the morning room and took advantage of that time to run her errands and to also pick up a few Christmas gifts. She was excited about the gift she was planning for Jason and eagerly anticipated Christmas Eve with him and waking up next to him on Christmas morning. She planned to go to New York for Christmas since Mona was not around to spend the holidays with and she was sure that Sam would be with Rich. She had spoken with Agnes and offered to help her prepare Christmas dinner, but she had already arranged to have the small dinner catered, which had become their tradition, for the five of them, including Jason's daughter.

She was sure that, after the romantic pre-proposal last weekend, he would officially propose to her on Christmas Eve or at his parent's Christmas dinner. She was aware of how much they meant to him and she was excited to become a part of their family. Life was finally smiling on her in the romance category and she was grateful.

Giving him space must have been exactly what he needed because he was back to normal when Joya returned from her errands and said that he was looking forward to dinner with Sam and Rich. Joya and Sam arranged for the couples to meet for an early dinner since the weather was cold and unpredictable. Rich and Jason hit it off right away, having similar careers and interests. They identified mutual colleagues from their professional financial circle and made a date to play golf together in the Spring.

Joya and Sam exchanged satisfied glances between them that the men in their lives connected, Joya thinking that they made a great foursome and hoped that Sam would continue to see Rich so they could enjoy more times like this.

Chapter 64

Rich enjoyed dinner with Joya and Jason, but was looking forward to getting home with Sam. Just watching her eat dinner had turned him on and distracted him from the conversation with Jason more than a few times. Sam knew what she was doing and he loved the secret flirtation between them. Joya and Jason didn't seem to notice.

He had always liked big women, but Sam was his first plus sized African American woman. After being with her, it was confirmed for him: now that he had gone black, he would never go back. He wanted to marry Sam, but she was not having it. He was determined to wear her down.

After dinner and as soon as they were in his Jaguar in the parking garage, he kissed her hard, his tongue almost down her throat and his hand under her dress and inside her panties. He could feel that she was as aroused as he was.

"I can't wait to get your delicious ass home," he whispered in her ear. "You are such a tease, but I love it. You are going to love what I have planned for you."

"What are we waiting for?" Sam moaned. "Let's get going before we have to do it in the car like two teenagers in heat."

Not like we haven't done it before, Rich relished the thought, but withdrew his hand from under her dress, gave her his sexy smile and drove home, careful not to break any speed limits since he had been drinking. Once they arrived to his townhome and were inside, Sam pressed her weight against his average sized frame, ready for him to finish what he started in the car.

"No, my darling," he said as he turned her towards the living room. "You have to finish what you started with me during dinner. You made me so hot for you when you were eating," he said through gritted teeth. "Come," he said as he led her to the sunken living room. She sank down into the sofa and he reached behind the pillow cushion for a silk scarf that he left there the last time that she was over. He gently tied it around her eyes while licking her neck. She moaned with pleasure, anticipating what was to come.

"Wait here, my sweet. I'll be right back."

Sam stripped off her clothes and was completely naked and ready for Rich when he returned. The first scent he waved in front of her nose was sweet, delectable and familiar. She was sure she knew what it was, but waited for his instruction. "Bite, my sweet," he instructed as he placed the sweetness to her lips.

She opened her mouth and bit down on the rich white chocolate covered strawberry, enjoying the juiciness inside her mouth as Rich licked the juice on her lips. He put the second piece of chocolate fruit in his mouth, sharing it with Sam by way of a deeply passionate kiss. The sound of their harmonious groans conveyed their shared pleasure.

It was only a few minutes before they simultaneously exploded in the ecstasy of the blended decadence of food and sex. Watching Sam eat was foreplay for Rich and she loved playing food games with him. He always had a special treat for her before, after and often times during sex.

At least for the present time, she didn't care about the weight gain.

The bigger she became, the more he wanted her.

Chapter 65

"Merry Christmas, ma'am," the doorman said to Joya, as he swiftly opened the door for her. He recognized her as Mr. White's girlfriend and didn't hesitate to allow her access to the apartment building.

Yeah – right – Merry Christmas – whatever, Joya thought sarcastically, but didn't say it the way she was thinking it. "Thank you; Merry Christmas," she answered the polite doorman. Her heart pounded as she rode the elevator to the penthouse apartment. Jason had not answered any of her calls since his last visit when she noticed his mood shift. He hadn't kept his ritual of calling in the morning and evening. He sent a couple of text messages that he was busy and would talk later. Later never came.

They had planned to spend Christmas together, so Joya took the train Christmas morning instead of Christmas Eve as she had originally planned. Maybe he was planning a surprise for their engagement and she didn't want to be in the way. That was the romantic dreamer in her, but her gut and intuition were informing her differently, although she didn't want to acknowledge it. She would now come face-to-face with whatever was preventing Jason's communication with her.

She wasn't sure what she would discover upon arriving at Jason's apartment, and the negative thoughts prevailed. *Another woman? A man, perhaps? Sickness? What?* She took a deep breath and rang the doorbell. She wouldn't use her key unless she absolutely had to. She listened for movement and thought she heard something. She waited a few more seconds, and then rang the bell again. This time, she was sure that she heard him - or someone, walking inside. But, she still stood there waiting.

She tapped on the door with her knuckles. "Jason! It's me – Joya. Please open the door." Jason reluctantly opened the door. Joya was shocked when she saw that he was not dressed, still in his pajama bottoms and t-shirt. He hadn't shaved, his hair had not been combed and looked like he had missed his weekly barber appointment. He stepped back to let Joya in, but did not make eye contact with her. He closed the door and retreated to living room, now unable to avoid the confrontation that he knew was inevitable.

"Jason – what's wrong, honey?" she asked as she sat next to the man she hardly recognized.

He drew a deep breath, "I just needed some time alone to sort things out for myself."

"Things? What things? What's bothering you?"

"Just some personal things, Joya!" he retorted. "I just need some time. Is that too much to ask?"

"No, it's not too much to ask, Jason – if you had ASKED instead of ignoring my phone calls and cutting off communication with me. And, it's Christmas. We are supposed to have dinner with your parents today."

"I told them we couldn't make it," he said.

"Without talking to me about it? I've been worried about you for the past two weeks. Why wouldn't you talk to me?"

"I told you – I need some time," he said staring at the floor.

She touched his shoulder, "Won't you tell me what's bothering you? Jason – look at me, please. Please talk to me. Tell me what's in your head. Tell me what's in your heart."

No response.

"Did I do something? Am I a part of whatever is bothering you?" she asked, almost afraid of the answer.

"No," he answered, still not looking up.

Truly afraid of the answer to the next question, but she had to know, "Are you seeing someone else?" she asked.

"No."

Joya's heart was pounding in her throat and she feared that she would puke, but she would not leave until she had the answers to her questions. "Do you want to continue our relationship?"

No answer.

"Jason? Please answer me," Joya begged.

Jason continued to stare at the floor and did not answer. Her eyes filled with tears as she re-phrased the question. "Do you want to stop seeing me?" He looked up at her then, unaffected by her emotion and the visible tears running down her cheeks.

"Can we still be friends?" he asked.

Joya's heart had been broken before and she thought that she could survive anything after Keith, but she was wrong. Jason had restored her hope and faith in love, and had become her best friend and the focus of her world. She wanted to be his wife and the daughter-in-law to his parents, and step-mother to his daughter. She felt her entire world crumble and her heart fragmented into a million tiny little pieces.

Yet again.

"Jason, you asked me to MARRY you! What was that all about? How do we go from planning a life together to casual friendship?"

Joya was confused, hurt and dejected by Jason's request to be friends. Through her tears, she straightforwardly reminded him that, "At a minimum, FRIENDS are honest with each other and share with each other. FRIENDS communicate with each other. FRIENDS return phone calls and text messages. You won't even tell me what's wrong. That's not what FRIENDS do. That's not what two people IN LOVE do. You are probably the smartest person that I know, but you missed the lesson on friendship."

She still received no response from him, so she wiped her face and reached in her pocket for the keys to his apartment, placing them on the coffee table in front of him – a symbol of finality. *Please stop me. Tell me this is not real.* The more she talked without a response from Jason, the angrier she became and her pained feelings intensified. Asking to be her friend, after asking her to be his wife felt like a betrayal and a devaluation of her feelings for him and what she was prepared to accept to be his wife. Joya retaliated the only way she could – with words.

She stood to her feet, slung her purse onto her shoulder and looked down at him still sitting on the sofa. She repeated his question. "Can we be friends? Yes, Jason, we can be friends – just not friends with each other."

Chapter 66

God, are you playing a cruel trick on me? Or is this just my karma? Why me? What have I done to deserve having my heart broken again? Joya turned her head towards the window, closed her eyes, and replayed her confrontation with Jason. After rewinding the scene over and over, she opened her eyes hoping that she would awaken from the nightmare. Instead, she saw the familiar reflection of sadness and anguish staring back at her, questioning why Jason had come into her life only to leave. And, to leave without explanation. It must be her punishment, but punishment for what?

She was glad that she had a seat to herself in the Quiet Car on the Amtrak having arrived at the station just in time to catch the next train back to D.C. She took a deep breath and said a silent prayer for Jason. In spite of her own pain and confusion, she felt that he needed something – she just wasn't sure what it was that he needed.

I'm giving up on men and the hope of a meaningful relationship. I bet that crazy Bob Jones is somewhere with his harem of women and about one hundred children, all running around looking just like him, Joya flashed back to the many years ago when she thought she had found her first "Prince Charming."

Bob Jones was indeed surrounded by his many clone-like children on this Christmas day. He married one of the "baby-mamas" and they had two more children together. All of his children were at his house celebrating the holiday. He hadn't thought of Joya in many years.

Keith is probably somewhere cheating on his wife. I loved him so much; probably still do, Joya continued to reflect. *Despite everything, he truly was my soulmate.* She released an audible breath of disappointment, wishing that things could have turned out differently for her and Keith.

Keith was in the Kentlands, an upscale Maryland community, having Christmas dinner with his cookie-cutter wife and her parents, smiling and faking it while thinking about and longing for Joya. He never stopped loving her and regretted that she saw him that evening with his most recent extra-marital affair. He never loved anyone except Joya and wanted to tell her – if he ever had the chance. He wondered what Christmas would be like with Joya...

Troy is probably somewhere banging Rod, Joya laughed at the thought.

Troy kissed his daughter goodbye after spending an hour with her on Christmas day. Her mother always allowed him to see his daughter and wished that he would spend more time with her, but she knew that Troy was Troy – selfish. He sent Rod a text message from the car confirming their trip to Atlantic

City in the morning. He wanted to know if he had booked the prostitutes.

David….maybe I should have chosen David. He is a good man, but would he cheat on me, too? What if? Joya shook her head in self-disgust at the irony of her last words to David requesting for them to be friends after she announced to him that her future was with another.

David walked alongside his children to see the Christmas trees at the White House. He made the effort to see them every day to establish a semblance of normalcy. They seemed happy. Everyone, including Lynn, seemed happy. Everyone was happy except David. He wondered where Joya was and what she was doing. He thought that she was probably with the lucky guy she told him she was planning to marry. He wished things had worked out for him and Joya, but accepted that it was not meant to be. He vowed to find happiness in the year ahead.

Jason…Jason, my love – what happened? We were so happy. What's going on with you?

Jason was on the phone talking to his doctor's answering service, explaining that he needed to be seen immediately. He was having an episode. He'd stopped taking his meds to control his bipolar disorder, hoping that it would resolve his impotence. His doctor had strongly advised him against it, but he wanted to be a man in every way for Joya. The little blue pill gave him headaches, made him feel sick and may have been contraindicated because of his other meds. At this point, he didn't know which was worse – his bipolar condition, his impotence or having just lost Joya. He should have been honest with her about his illness, but what would she think...

He should have given her the chance to decide.

Chapter 67

What a Christmas – the worst one ever, Joya thought as she walked out of her office building to take a stroll the day before New Year's Eve. It was dusk and the cold wind had already wrapped around her. She completed her work for the day and just wanted to get some exercise and fresh air. She didn't have a destination in mind; she just wanted – and needed - to clear her head.

What doesn't kill you makes you stronger, the adage echoed her thoughts as she continued to walk the side streets of the National Harbor. She was recovering from the shock of Jason's sudden and unexplained behavior that led to their break up. Although not the first man to disappoint her or to break her heart, she was more resilient this time around. She spent a couple of days after the unpleasant incident allowing the tears to flow and the emotion to rise so that she could manage them. After talking to Mona and Sam about it, she felt better, but still didn't understand. Only Jason could explain what was happening, but he didn't call and she resolved not to call him. It was over as far as Joya was concerned.

Mona, still living in Paris, had not met Jason, but heard all about him from Joya. She told Joya that she was sorry that it didn't work out with them, but that she had to trust that it was better that it happened on "this side of the ring" instead of after they were married. Joya agreed. Mona reassured her by reminding her, "Let him find you, Joya. The right man is out there for you and he WILL find you. Just be patient."

Sam confessed that there was something about Jason that she couldn't quite put her finger on, but she was supportive and hopeful for them, always wanting the best for her best friend.

Joya inhaled the frigid air, allowing it to fill her lungs. Visibly seeing her breath on the exhale, she symbolically released the bitterness and disappointment she had been feeling onto the white mist as it dissipated in front of her. It would still take some time for a full emotional recovery, but in the moment, the act was cathartic, liberating and exactly what she needed.

The Waterfront Haven loomed in the distance – her favorite restaurant. She suddenly remembered Bryce inviting her to a celebration for the staff and special customers and thought that it was today. She wasn't sure if it was today and if she was dressed properly, but decided to go in and check it out. She could use some gaiety to offset the doom and gloom of how the holiday had gone for her so far.

Joya received the answer as soon as she reached the door of the restaurant. The sign read, 'Closed for Private Party.' She looked in through the window for Bryce or Terri. Bryce saw her walking towards the restaurant and was already making his way to the door to greet her.

"Hey! You remembered. I'm glad that you came! Come on in," he said holding the door open for her. Joya didn't confess that she didn't remember, but that it was more happenstance. In any event, she was glad that she did think of it. The atmosphere was exactly what she needed. She recognized the staff and most of the customers who were also regulars. Everyone was eating, drinking, laughing and having a good time. She didn't need to worry about whether she was dressed appropriately because the restaurant staff was dressed casually and most of the customers were dressed like her, also coming straight from work or their homes.

Bryce led her to the buffet and invited her to help herself while he stepped away to mix her favorite drink. He returned with her signature Kir Royale without the lemon twist, which she gratefully accepted with a smile. He liked her smile and his heart fluttered every time, although he didn't want to admit it or accept it. He admired Joya and enjoyed talking to her. She always made him laugh even when she was visibly stressed. He thought back to their 'non-date' to the winery and also the train trip to New York when they sat together. Something about being next to her felt so right, yet he kept his promise to himself to keep his heart closed. One heartbreak per lifetime was more than enough for him and plus, she told him more than once that she was involved with Jason.

Bryce guided Joya to a bar table by the window that had a perfect view of the Potomac, brilliantly reflecting multi-colored lights from the Ferris wheel that loomed above it. Joya sipped her drink, wondering about Jason. Bryce noticed her pensive look and she didn't hear his question, so he asked her again, "Joya - did you enjoy your holidays?"

"Not really," she answered honestly, but not offering additional details.

"Oh..." Bryce reacted, not expecting that answer from her. She was happy and excited when they rode the train to New York just a few short weeks ago. As he recalled, she was planning to spend the holidays with her man, Jason.

"I'm sorry to hear that," he said. Is everything okay with you?" He started to ask if everything was okay with her and Jason, but if he was being honest with himself, even though he was unsure why, he hoped that Jason was out of the picture. He saw them together once in the restaurant and he didn't seem like the right guy for a woman like Joya, appearing way too staunch and uptight for such a free-spirited woman.

"I'm good," she answered still distantly staring at the light display over the Potomac.

"The Ferris wheel looks beautiful over the water, especially during the holidays, don't you think?" The National Wheel was always in place at the end of the dock for riders to enjoy, but there was a special light display for the holidays, transitioning between red, gold, green, blue, and white.

"It does," Joya said. Bryce instinctively grabbed her hand. "Come with me," he invited. "Bring your drink," he instructed, grabbing his beer with his free hand.

"Okay, but where are we going?" She asked following him to the rear of the restaurant.

"I want to show you a better view of the holiday lights," he said reaching the first step of the spiral staircase leading to the owner's private dining area and office suite. Joya hesitated, remembering what he'd told her a while back about the top floor being a private area for the boss. "What's wrong?" Bryce asked.

"Is it okay for us to be up there? I thought you told me before that it's a private area for the owner of the restaurant. Where is he, by the way?" she asked curiously.

Bryce shook his head at beautiful Joya. *Always jumping to conclusions. Here we go again; I thought you knew by now...* "Come on," he tugged her hand.

They reached the upper level private dining room, spacious enough for a decent size mingling and standing party and with enough seating for twenty to thirty guests to comfortably enjoy a sit-down meal.

"There you go, my friend, drawing your own conclusions - yet again," Bryce jokingly accused her as he led her to the end of the hall. He stopped in front of the closed mahogany door, with the brass nameplate that read 'Bryce Simms.' "I am the boss," he reported. "I own this restaurant. And three others," he finished with a satisfied smile.

Chapter 68

He laughed at the embarrassment showing on Joya's flushed face. "I can't believe that you thought I was, as you say - the 'Bar Manager', all this time," he chuckled while Joya remained speechless. They stepped into his small, but lavishly decorated office that featured a windowed wall overlooking the Potomac. He was right, the view was spectacular. Joya stepped over to the window where she could see the traffic on the Wilson Bridge was beginning to become congested. It seemed that the red and white lights from the vehicles slowly moving in both directions across the bridge span were a part of the Harbor holiday light display.

She placed her drink on the nearby table and folded her arms across her chest, contemplating the past year and the year ahead. As badly as she felt about her breakup with Jason, the lights appeared as a symbol of hope for brighter days ahead. Bryce was conscious of her mood change. He stood next to her, also admiring the view. He saw it every day, but never took for granted.

"So – how do you like the view from here?" he asked.

"It's beautiful; just as you promised."

YOU are beautiful, Bryce thought as he looked down on Joya's profile in the soft light. He noticed her the first time that he saw her in the restaurant and always thought that she was an attractive, powerful business woman. In the time that he spent talking to her one-on-one, he learned of her inner beauty, her humor and tenacity. She is the type of woman that he would want to be with IF he wanted to be with another woman after having his heart broken.

"Penny for your thoughts?" he asked with a smile.

She returned the smile, remembering the last man that asked her that question – David. Thinking of David had no effect on her anymore, so she chuckled and answered Bryce. "I was thinking that the lights are a symbol of hope and good things to come. I wish that Christmas could last all year, but if it did, then it wouldn't be special, would it?" she asked for confirmation.

"You're right. Christmas has already become so commercialized, I hesitate to think of what would happen if it extended beyond the season as we know it," he laughed. "What about the new year ahead? Any plans or resolutions?" he curiously posed.

"My plans for the year drastically changed – without notice, I might add - last week. But, it's okay. I can switch gears. I've done it before," she smiled assuredly. "I'm going to follow the advice of my wise sister, and stop looking so hard for certain things and allow them to find me." Bryce wanted her to continue, now that his interest was piqued, but she turned the question back to him. "What about you, 'Mr. Restaurant Mogul?' I can't believe that I didn't know that you own this restaurant. I'm probably your BEST customer," she kidded, punching his shoulder.

Bryce laughed with her, answering her question, "I want to continue to be successful in business and fair to my employees. Looking deeply into her eyes, he added, "You probably are my best customer." She returned his gaze and an inexplicable and unforeseeable attraction formed between them. He moved cautiously closer to her.

Joya wasn't sure where the next question came from, but she asked him anyway, "What about your heart? Will you make it available to a woman worthy of your love?"

Open my heart? If I open my heart for you, will you come in? Would you love me or hurt me? Bryce considered her question with a few of his own. Her eyes reflected someone who experienced love, loss and pain, but also the desire and courage to love again. He didn't have the desire – until now and not sure if he was brave enough. He surrendered to the enchantment of the moment, not knowing if it would ever come again.

He softly touched her cheek. She impulsively placed her hand on top of his, moving closer to him. She thought it was too soon to be attracted to another so shortly after her heartbreak, but her inner voice was saying, *"Maybe I'm being found."*

Bryce wanted to ask Joya if she would be careful with his heart. "Can I ask you something?" Joya had a question of her own: *Have you been looking for me?* But, she would let him ask his question first.

"Yes – what would you like to ask me?" Mesmerized and magnetized to each other, Bryce willing lowered his head towards Joya's lips. He rested there, a breath away, still not sure. It was only a second before the sudden and unforeseen mystical power took over. He still wanted to ask his question, but instead their lips met in a soft kiss. They separated and looked into each other's eyes, both with their questions not yet verbalized.

Destiny designed this moment precisely for them, bringing them to this point in time, surrounding them in the dazzling lights that had become more vivid, only to the two of them. They were aware that the shared sensation of honesty and fate of their private, reserved instance was not a coincidence, but providence - to which they decided to surrender.

Joya was the first to speak, "I need you to repeat the question," she smiled sweetly. Bryce, having not said a word since he sought her permission to ask her the question he still had not asked, understood her invitation to repeat the question and reunited his lips to hers.

They would ask their questions later.

Or maybe they already had their answers.

Thank You

Thank you for reading my book. Your feedback is very important to me as I read all of the reviews for my books. I would very much appreciate it if you would leave an honest review for this and my other books on amazon.com.

If you would like to join my mailing list, or order my other books, please visit my website:
www.readellenora.com
or e-mail me: elle@readellenora.com

www.ingramcontent.com/pod-product-compliance
Lightning Source LLC
Chambersburg PA
CBHW070601130626
46556CB00001B/237